The Bombshell and the Bodyguard

The Bombshell and the Bodyguard

A SMALL TOWN BEST FRIEND'S SISTER ROMANCE

AN EASTPORT BAY BILLIONAIRES NOVEL

TRU TAYLOR

Contents

About

THE BOMBSHELL AND THE BODYGUARD

Meet the Bombshell...

I've kissed a lot of frogs. Not proud of it, and it's earned me some unflattering tabloid headlines... *Jade Leaves Another One Jaded.* But hey, at least I've gotten a string of hit songs out of the experience. And I've learned a lot from my highly public and lightning-fast relationships—namely what I *don't* want in a man.

So when my older brother's bad-boy best friend Wilder Lowe strolls back into my life, looking even more handsome, more dangerous, and *less* interested than ever, I don't give him a second glance.

Problem is, this time I can't just walk away—my billion-dollar pop-career has attracted its share of stalkers—the latest is the scariest one yet—and Wilder is my new bodyguard.

Meet the Bodyguard...

I'm not in the habit of turning down billionaires as potential clients. I didn't build my own immensely successful security business by being stupid.

But when my best friend asks me to act as a bodyguard for his very-much-forbidden little sister—you better believe I plan to turn down the detail. As a former Navy combat diver, a Frogman, I know a nuclear depth bomb when I see one.

Then there's a call in the middle of the night, and when I hear that frightened, all-too-familiar voice, the plea from the one girl I could never say no to, I'm lost. I'll do anything and everything it takes to keep her safe.

Even if that means whisking her away to my own private island.

The Bombshell and the Bodyguard is a hot small-town rom com take on The Frog Prince fairytale. It's a standalone secret crush/best friend's little sister/celebrity/bodyguard forbidden love story filled with heart, heat, and billionaire romance fun!

*A note from Tru: This book, like all the books in the Eastport Bay Billionaires series, can stand alone, and the series can be read in any order, but these modern fairytale retellings are interconnected in ways that make it fun to read them together. Welcome to Eastport Bay and enjoy the read!

MORE FROM EASTPORT BAY

Bookworm and the Beast- A Beauty and the Beast story
Bargain with the Bachelor- A Snow White story
The Baby and the Blueblood- A Cinderella story
The Baby-whisperer and the Brute- A Rapunzel story
The Bombshell and the Bodyguard- A Frog Prince story
Scarlett and the Big Bad Billionaire— A Red Riding Hood and the Big Bad Wolf story

The Grumpy Billionaire- A Sleeping Beauty story (Reid's story)
The Merry Billionaire— A holiday novella (Hap's story)
The Sleepless Billionaire- (Tuck's story) Free when you join my VIP list!

ONE
An Interesting Homecoming

You don't know temptation until you've spent a month alone on an island with the most fascinating woman you've ever known—who's also your best friend's little sister. —Wilder Lowe

Jessica

"Jade, Jade, Jade, Jade..."

The appreciative roar of the audience still echoed in my ears as I made my way from the stage through the back corridors of Gillette Stadium toward the artists' exit/entrance where my brother waited to pick me up.

I was so ready to collapse into the warm leather seat of his car and close my eyes. Live shows took every ounce of energy out of me—I always left everything on stage when performing.

The Boston show was the final one on my two-year concert tour, and at this point I was beyond exhausted.

Pushing open the heavy metal door, I spotted Hap's idling Lamborghini. He gave me a wave from the driver's seat, and relief spread through me like a cool stream of air on a sweltering day.

At least a couple dozen fans also waited in the narrow alleyway, crying out my stage name and holding t-shirts and hats and magazines with my face on them.

"Jade will you sign this?"

"I love you Jade. You're my favorite singer of all time."

Many of them stretched their hands out toward me or held out gifts or items they wanted me to autograph.

My heart squeezed, and I got a new burst of energy. My fans were literally the *best*. There was *no way* I would duck my head and run for the waiting car.

I'd have plenty of time to rest once I got to Eastport Bay. As soon as I got there, I'd slide into my own bed in my own home.

Heaven. I might stay under the covers for a week. Or two.

Would Uber eats bring the food directly to my bedroom?

Unable to ignore the insistent throbbing of my feet, I kicked off the uncomfortable platform heels I'd performed in and walked over to the line security had roped off to hold the fans back.

"Hi. What's your name?" A girl who appeared to be about thirteen stood smiling and crying at the same time, clutching a concert t-shirt.

"Hannah," she answered. "I love you so much."

Again, my heart contracted. I hugged her. "I love you, too. Thank you for coming to my show."

She wrapped her arms around me and squeezed hard then asked me to sign the shirt. When I was done, I took a selfie with her and moved to the next person.

"Hi. Did you have a good time tonight?"

"Yes. I loved it. It was such a good show. I wish I could see it again tomorrow night."

This girl looked about sixteen and was accompanied by several friends. Seeing them laughing and chattering together made me smile—it also reminded me of what I'd given up to become a child performer at about their age.

"You all look great tonight," I told them. "Let's take a group shot, okay?"

One of the security personnel from the venue held the camera for us as we made silly faces and poses.

When they'd left happy, I signed an autograph for a man who literally didn't say a word to me. He just looked down at my bare feet the whole time. Shy, I guessed.

"Thanks for coming tonight," I said.

I moved down the line, offering personal greetings and photo ops to everyone who'd cared enough to wait around and see me after my show.

When I'd spent a few minutes with each of them and felt like I literally couldn't stay on my feet another minute, I started looking around for my shoes.

Weird. They were gone.

"Did any of you pick up my shoes?" I asked the security staff.

They looked at each other then at me, shaking their heads.

"Well, okay then. I guess they're gone. I'm probably going to find someone selling vials of 'Jade's authentic foot odor' on eBay." I joked. "Goodnight guys. Thanks for everything."

Pulling open the passenger door of Hap's car, I dropped inside.

"Hey there Kermit." My big brother's nickname for me.

When we were kids, I'd hated it—he'd claimed my vivid green eyes reminded him of a frog. But now the good-natured taunt and the familiar sound of his voice only made me smile.

I'm home.

"Hey there *Bobby*," I said as payback, calling him by his hated childhood nickname. It had been replaced by the stage name Happy and later shortened to Hap, which he'd liked enough to keep in real life.

He started the ignition and gave me the same dimpled grin that had melted the hearts of tweens everywhere back when he'd been the star of Happy's Family.

The weekly series had run for nine years on network TV, earning him an Emmy award, a Golden Globe, and enough money to keep him in comfort the rest of his life. The residuals from syndication of the reruns were probably enough to fund the state budget of Rhode Island where we both lived.

"Caught most of the show," Hap said. "You sounded great. I almost forget you're my baby sister when you're up there—I just get into the music."

"Thanks. I'm shocked I even have a voice left after two years on the road. Please remind me never to sign on for such a long tour ever again."

"I will... but you'll do it anyway," he teased. "You're the hardest-working billionaire I know."

I laughed. "I seriously doubt that. Didn't your former roommates specifically move in together so they could work round the clock on Chipp?"

Until recently, Hap had lived with six of his closest friends from high school. Together they'd rented a subdivided mansion on Eastport Bay's glamorous Oceanview Avenue, living and working there while the others all prepared for the launch of a new software company and Hap got his TV producing and directing career going.

The unconventional living arrangement had earned them the dubious nickname of the Seven Dwarves among the locals.

"Yeah, I guess you're right," Hap said. "Maybe what I meant to say is that *I'm* the *laziest* billionaire I know. But I *am* an excellent chauffeur."

"That you are." I grinned. "Seriously, though, thanks for coming to get me. I'm *way* too tired to drive tonight."

"I'm surprised there wasn't some kind of party for the end of the tour."

"There was. After last night's show. Which is another reason I'm worn out. We barely slept last night. My body's about nine-eight percent Coke Zero right now."

"Okay caffeine queen, I'll have you home in an hour and a half, but feel free to doze on the way there if you need to."

"I might not be able to help it," I said apologetically. "I'm glad mom and Dad won't be home from their cruise till Tuesday because I might just sleep until then."

I must have fallen asleep because I was awakened sometime later by Hap's voice.

"What the hell?"

The alarm in his tone had me alert in an instant. I sat up, looking around in the darkness. "What is it? Where are we?"

"At your house. Something's wrong." He pointed at the windshield, indicating the scene outside.

There were squad cars parked along the street outside the gates of my estate and two inside of it on the circular drive. All had lights flashing, though there were no sirens.

"What's going on?"

I started to open my door, but Hap held out his hand. "Stay here. I'm gonna go find out what's happening."

He got out of the car but leaned back into it, meeting my eyes. "Lock the doors. I'll be right back."

My gaze followed him as he jogged away and disappeared into the night. The wait for his return felt like hours, and my heart raced the entire time. I'd been ready to sleep for days, but now I felt wired, filled with fight-or-flight energy.

What was happening at my house?

My first thought was that there'd been a fire. But then there were no fire engines, only police cars. It had to be something else—a burglary maybe?

Chills went down my spine as I pictured breaking glass, a gloved hand slipping in and turning the back-door lock.

It wouldn't be the first time one of my homes had been

robbed. My house in California had been broken into a few months ago. Thankfully I'd been out of the country at the time, but it had still freaked me out.

What if I *had* been home tonight when a stranger had forced his way in? What if there was *still* an intruder in my house *right now*?

Oh, where was Hap? I peered down the long, dark driveway, searching for a glimpse of my brother. Finally I saw him, striding quickly toward the car.

He got inside, and before I could even say anything, he said, "You're staying with me tonight."

He put the car in drive and pulled it away from the curb, a determined look on his face.

"Was it a break-in?" I asked his profile. Cold, spiky alarm clogged my throat, preventing me from saying more.

"Apparently. Attempted one at least. The police think the alarm probably scared him off. They're checking just to make sure the house wasn't breached and that there isn't still somebody hanging around. After that, they'll spread out and canvas the neighborhood, but the houses are so far apart, I doubt anyone saw anything. I gave them my number to call when it's all clear, but you're not sleeping there tonight."

"You won't get an argument from me on that one. Will Rachel be okay with me staying over? I could go to Mom and Dad's house. I've still got my key."

"Don't be silly. Rachel loves you. We're all family now."

I'd only met Hap's new bride once—at their destination wedding in Hawaii. The two of us had gotten along famously, and I'd never seen my brother so happy.

That was all I cared about really. Rachel and I could have been polar opposites and I'd still be her biggest fan as long as she treated my brother right.

She was waiting at the door when we arrived. He'd obviously texted her to give her a heads up, because she reached for me and folded me into her arms.

"Oh my goodness. You must be so upset—and so tired. This was the last thing you needed on the last night of your tour."

"It's an interesting homecoming, that's for sure," I said. "Thanks for letting me stay tonight—I know you weren't expecting it."

"Don't be silly. I'm thrilled to see you. And you can stay as long as you like. I don't want you going back to that house until we know it's completely safe."

Hap nodded in agreement. "You need to beef up your security."

Hap had always been overprotective, and no doubt this incident sent his big-brother instincts into overdrive. I attempted to set his mind at ease.

"I already have a watchman at the gate and a security guard on the grounds. After the California incident my record label hired them to watch my property while I'm on tour."

"Well, you're not on tour anymore. You're home now. Which means there'll be something much more valuable there than pricey art and platinum records on the wall—*you*."

He pulled a phone from his pocket. "I've got a friend in the security business. I'm gonna give him a call, get him to go take a look and—"

The phone in Hap's hand buzzed, cutting him off. He looked up at Rachel and me. "It's the police."

Lifting the phone to his ear, he said, "Hello? Yeah. Yeah, okay. She's right here." He held it out to me. "They want to talk to you."

The officer on the other end of the line told me they'd checked the entire nine acres of my estate but had found no signs of an intruder. "Sometimes these alarm systems are tricky. Even a strong gust of wind can set them off," he explained.

I thanked him and dialed Gordon, the security guard assigned to my property. After apologizing profusely—for what I wasn't sure—he told me he hadn't seen or heard anything unusual before the alarm went off and reiterated what the police officer had said.

"I don't think this was the same as that situation in California, Miss Bailey. It might have been a bat or a bird that flew into one of the windowpanes—or like the police said, the wind. There's a storm system off the coast tonight, so it's higher than usual."

"Okay. That's good." The tension drained from my shoulders. "As long as no one got in."

"No. No ma'am, there are no signs of that. There are some curiosity seekers who come by the property and peek through the gates, but I always keep them well off the grounds."

"Okay well, I feel better. Thanks, Gordon. I'm spending the night at my brother's house, but I'll be home in the morning."

When I ended the call, Hap was staring at me, and he didn't look pleased. "I don't think that's a good idea. I want my guy to check the place out before you go home."

His face was painted with concern, but I was no longer worried. "Everything's fine. The police and the security guard think it was most likely the wind that set off the alarm. There weren't any signs of forced entry or even someone on the grounds. Anyway, we can talk about it tomorrow. I'm so tired I can hardly think."

Rachel took over, coming to wrap an arm around me and guide me toward the staircase. Her touch and tone were comforting, almost motherly.

"Of course you are. You don't need to think about anything tonight except getting a good night's sleep. I've got a guest room ready for you. There are towels and shampoo and soap and everything in the adjoining bath. Want anything to eat before you go to bed?"

"No. I'm too tired to eat, too."

"Okay, well I'll make you anything you want for breakfast and plenty of it," she promised.

In spite of what I'd just said, my stomach released a low growl. Rachel was a professional chef. Anything she made was bound to be delicious.

Realizing I hadn't said goodnight to my brother, I stopped at the foot of the stairs and turned back toward him. "Thanks for everything—for coming to get me, for giving me a place to stay..."

Hap's mood hadn't improved in the past minute. The pensive look was still on his face. "You don't have to thank me. I'm just glad you're here—and that you're safe. Goodnight Jess."

"Goodnight Hap."

As I trudged up the stairs beside his wife, I had little doubt that the minute we were out of earshot, my brother would pull out his phone again and dial his friend at the security firm.

Honestly, I was too tired to worry about it. And what did I care which company handled my home security?

One was probably as good as the next, and in any case, I'd deal with it tomorrow.

TWO
Teaser

Jessica

The first thing I did upon waking the next morning was go to the bedroom's wall of windows and open the heavy drapes.

Sunlight streamed in, and a smile settled across my lips. I sighed with pleasure. There it was—the gorgeous deep blue of the Atlantic.

I'd traveled all over the world, but *this* view... this was the one I loved most.

It was the main reason I'd bought my own home not far from here. Unlike Hap's house, it wasn't on prestigious Oceanview Avenue but on Atlantic Avenue and was situated directly on the open ocean with breathtaking views from every room.

Majestic but also comforting, the ocean was part of my earliest memories, of running across damp sand with bare feet, gathering shells and rocks and hermit crabs in a bucket, of bracing cold water contrasting with the hot summer sun.

And the fresh briny smell was all things good—sailing,

swimming, walks along the shoreline dreaming of what my future might hold.

I opened a window to let in a breeze then shivered, remembering it was only Spring here—international travel tended to mess up not only my internal clock and sleep schedule but also made it hard to keep track of the seasons. I'd performed in Australia and New Zealand before flying back to the U.S. for my shows in New York and Boston.

Shutting the window again, I showered and dressed then went downstairs where I was met with a surprise. The kitchen's breakfast nook was filled with men.

They weren't strangers. I'd known all of them since I was a girl, though I hadn't seen them since my brother's wedding.

Hap's high school buddies had become his housemates at the billionaire bachelor house and then his groomsmen. Now they sat around the table laughing, talking, and stuffing their mouths with Rachel's incredible cooking,

And it did smell good. My empty stomach roared its protest as I made my way into the warm, bright, fragrant room.

Spotting me, a couple of the guys—Josh and Paul—jumped up and hugged me. Aiden kept his seat—even after all these years of knowing each other, he was too shy to greet me with anything but a quiet hello and a bashful smile. Even Reid, who'd moved out of the billionaire bachelor house and was sometimes a little grumpy and standoffish, was there.

"What are you guys all doing here?" I asked.

"Eating us out of house and home," Rachel quipped as she delivered a platter of hot pancakes and sizzling bacon to the table. Forks shot out to spear the replenishments.

Paul answered her question. "Hap *stole* our in-house chef."

"Yeah, so we *have* to come over here now if we want anything good to eat," Josh said.

Rachel had worked as a personal chef in Colorado before moving to Eastport Bay to be closer to family. She'd taken a job at the billionaire bachelor house cooking all the guys' meals—that was where she and Hap had met. Last fall she'd opened her own fine dining restaurant in a renovated rum distillery in Eastport Bay's harbor district.

Apparently she was taking a day off today, since on a normal workday she'd already be out of the house and at the fish market and produce stands securing the freshest local ingredients for her menu.

Hap entered the kitchen, coming up behind his wife and wrapping his arms around her waist. He tossed a verbal barb over his shoulder.

"Your loss is my gain, suckers. You're either going to have to learn to fend for yourselves in the kitchen—or find your own chef to marry."

"I'm never getting married," Josh said. "We hardly see you and Hunter and Tuck anymore—your wives never let you out of the house."

Hap gave a silly eyebrow waggle. "Maybe we don't *want* to leave the house."

His overdone lecherous tone elicited a giggle from Rachel and a playful slap at his arm.

"You dating anyone at the moment, Jess?" Reid teased. "Maybe I'll marry a beautiful, rich pop star and let *her* pay for a personal chef."

"Hey—" Hap barked. "All of you losers stay away from my baby sister. Not a one of you is good enough for her. And you —" He pointed at Reid in mock-threat. "You're probably richer than all of us put together at this point, so pay for your own damn chef."

Reid, who was my age—younger than the other guys—had not only helped to launch Chipp, but he'd started his own website that was sort of a blend between Facebook and a matchmaking service.

StillYours.com had helped to reunite millions of "young loves" across the globe and was the fastest growing social media site in the world.

Everyone laughed at Hap's remark, and I made myself a plate, enjoying the unexpected immersion in the family environment so alive here in my brother's home. My own house would seem awfully quiet when I went there later today—alone.

I would try not to think too hard about that. While fame delivered the the ultimate "popularity," inspiring throngs of strangers to feel a kinship to you and even declare their love, it was actually rather isolating.

Even reconnecting with high school friends might be an awkward proposition. Though we'd been close, I'd lost touch with them long ago after leaving school in the tenth grade to star in a TV show.

On the set of *Just Jade* in LA, I'd been surrounded by mostly adults and had spent all my time working and finishing high school with a private tutor. Now, I traveled so much that the people I did consider friends were scattered across the globe, and we kept in touch via phone and social media.

Well, you can't have it all.

I knew I was lucky. I had a career and lifestyle countless others would envy. I had more money than I could ever spend.

It was unreasonable to expect a stellar personal life as well. And true love... well, based on the way my love life had played out so far, that wasn't in the cards for me.

Hap made a plate and came to sit beside me at the table. "I asked my buddy to stop by your house this morning and check things out. He'll be here in a little while to meet with us."

"You didn't have to do that," I scolded gently. "I'm a big girl now, Hap. I can deal with my own security issues. I was planning to call my company today and have them post an additional guard."

"Uh-uh. You're firing that company," my brother said bluntly. "They failed. This guy's the best in the business. And he's a personal friend. I'd trust him with my life—and with yours. Anyway, he's already on his way over."

Oh no.

I worked hard to keep from gritting my teeth, though my nails bit into the flesh of my clenched palms. "Who is it?"

Please don't let it be him. Don't say Wilder.

"Wilder Lowe. Remember him?"

As if I could forget. *Of course* that was who Hap would call. Wilder ran an elite security firm based here in Eastport Bay.

More importantly, he'd been Hap's closest friend since middle school, the first person to befriend him when his sitcom had been canceled and our family had moved from Los Angeles to Eastport Bay.

Hap had always said Wilder was the most loyal person he'd ever met. They'd maintained their friendship during the years Wilder played college football and later when he'd served as a Navy SEAL.

"I don't think you've seen him since you left to go work on *Just Jade*," Hap said. "He used to come over to the house all the time—big guy, football player?"

Swallowing a lump in my throat, I nodded tightly. "I remember. Actually I saw him last year—at Sullivan Reece's wedding reception. He was in charge of security. We didn't talk much."

Understatement of the decade.

I'd invited Wilder out for a drink to catch up, and he'd shut me down cold, claiming his duties with the star-studded wedding would keep him busy the entire night and into the next morning right up until I was scheduled to fly out again.

Of course I'd recognized the excuse for what it was—Wilder Lowe had no more interest in the grown-up version of me than he'd had in the shy, awkward sixteen-year-old I'd been back when I'd carried an adolescent torch for him so bright he'd probably needed sunglasses whenever I was around.

Even now the memory of our brief exchange at the wedding reception caused my face to heat and my stomach to sink.

I can't believe I asked him out.

"Oh yeah, I forgot you flew in for that. Such a celebrity... jetting in and out in a day," Hap teased. "We little people barely got a glimpse of you."

I didn't laugh. I was concentrating too hard on keeping down the breakfast I'd just eaten. My stomach was a mass of raw nerves.

Wilder was on his way over. *Right now.*

Maybe it wasn't too late. Maybe I could tell Hap to call it off. Maybe—

The doorbell rang. Hap set down his fork and left the table, walking swiftly toward the front door. He turned back to shoot a glance over his shoulder.

"That'll be him. You finished?"

Though my plate was still half-full, I nodded and stood. I'd always had a nervous stomach and couldn't eat another bite now to save my life.

I deposited my plate in the sink, thanked Rachel for breakfast, then popped into the powder room to check my face before joining Hap in the foyer. I could just imagine greeting Wilder with a big ole blueberry stuck in my front teeth.

When I reached the foyer, Wilder had already come inside and was standing there with my brother, towering over him and making Hap's six-foot height look insignificant by comparison.

Of course *no one* could compare to Wilder Lowe. No one had ever come close.

He'd been six-foot-five by his sophomore year with thick, shiny hair and hazel eyes that had given eighth grade Jessica no end of song-writing inspiration.

Of course he'd been lankier back then, not nearly as filled-out and muscular as he was now, but to my mind, he'd been the most beautiful boy on earth.

And he'd been the best at everything—the best football player in our school and probably the entire state, a talented baseball player, a straight A student with a quick wit and even quicker smile.

It had gotten him out of more than a few incidences of "boyish mischief." He'd been idolized by all the guys and desired by all the girls.

I had been no exception. But I'd resigned myself to simply orbiting his magnetic sphere—close but always on the periphery. I'd stood no chance against the other girls vying for his attention, all of them prettier, older—and bolder.

As he'd spent so much time at our house with Hap, I'd made several futile attempts to capture his attention.

Once I thought I might actually have succeeded in making him see me as something other than his best friend's annoying little sister, but that golden moment had been long ago and hadn't lasted nearly as long as I'd wanted it to.

And it had been tarnished by the utter humiliation that had followed.

At least I'd gotten a hit song out of it—my first, in fact. "Teaser" had gone double-platinum and launched me into the upper echelon of the music industry.

He might barely notice me, but Wilder Lowe had played a crucial role in making me a star.

I doubted he even realized the song was about him. If he

did, it would take a lot of guts to stand there looking at me now with such a friendly, open smile on his face.

A new layer of steel coated my backbone, giving me the strength to stand a little taller.

Taking a deep, fortifying breath, I strode toward the two men and pasted on the stage-smile I relied upon when I was sick or exhausted and the show had to go on anyway.

"Hello Wilder. It's good to see you again."

THREE
Off-Limits

Wilder

Jessica, Hap and I sat in Hap's office, discussing home security.

It seemed surreal to be here like this, talking with her the way I'd talk with any other potential client, while inside, my heart and mind were participating in a riot—complete with looting, arson, and graffiti.

Stop Staring At Her was spray-painted in bright red across my brain, but my optic nerve couldn't seem to relay the message with all the noise.

"... so you can see why she needs a different security firm," Hap was saying.

I hoped I hadn't missed too much of the conversation.

"Right." I cleared my throat and attempted to do the same with my mind. "I did notice several deficiencies in the perimeter defense system. If you'd like, I'll put my home security expert Gray Lupine on it as soon as possible. He's a pro with a very... unique skill set. His qualifications are unmatched. Gray is out of state today, but he'll be back late tonight. We'll come by first thing Tuesday morning to do a thorough assessment."

Hap nodded, looking pleased and relaxing a bit in his leather club chair. "What about personal security? A bodyguard?"

"We can take care of that, too," I assured him. "No one understands wanting privacy better than I do. And as far as safety, everyone in my firm is a former SEAL. We're prepared for anything."

In the matching chair next to Hap, Jessica sat listening quietly. Her posture was relaxed and confident, but there was tension around her eyes and lips.

It felt a little strange to be discussing her home security needs with her brother instead of with her, but she hadn't said much at all since our initial exchange of polite greetings. Maybe she was too rattled from the alarm last night.

I forced myself to meet the unusual green eyes that had always drawn me in when I should have been looking the other way. "What do you think, Jessica? Sound good to you?"

A spark lit the jade-green irises. When she answered, an unexpected hint of disdain flavored her tone. "I'm still not sure it's necessary. It was a false alarm—there was no break-in. And do you even have time to take this on? I remember from when we spoke at the Reece wedding how *busy* you are."

Ah. So she wasn't rattled. She was pissed.

The moment I'd turned down her invitation to get a drink after the reception or to have breakfast the next morning and catch up, I'd known I'd hurt Jessica's feelings.

She saw me as her brother's best friend. She didn't understand my reluctance to spend any time with her.

She had no idea how I'd always felt about her—and that's how it would stay.

It hadn't been good for me to see her last year at the

wedding. I'd worked very hard over the years to forget about Jessica Bailey's effect on me.

I'd been (mostly) successful at putting her out of my mind, though it had been impossible to do completely with her alluring voice all over radio and her face on TV.

But seeing her at Sully and Angelina's wedding—in that silver evening gown—had snapped her right back to the forefront of my mind, and no matter how hard I tried to distract myself, she'd taken up residence there since that night.

And now she was sitting right in front of me, somehow looking even *more* appealing in a pair of jeans and a t-shirt, without a drop of makeup on.

Those incredible green eyes narrowed, awaiting my response. I had to give her one that wouldn't pique Hap's interest or alert him to the unspoken and long-running issue between his little sister and me.

Laughing lightly, I pretended to miss her surly tone. "Always. Good help is hard to find when you're dealing with the privacy and security of exclusive clientele, and as I said, we have exacting standards. I end up doing way too much of it myself. But you'll like Gray. And all my guys are the ultimate professionals. I have zero qualms about putting you in the hands of any one of my bodyguards."

And out of mine.

Hap straightened and sat forward. "Wait—no. I don't want one of your employees to do it. I want you to handle it."

Caught by surprise, I recoiled. "You want *me* to be her bodyguard?"

"Of course. I'm sure the guys who work for you are great, but you're the one I trust."

Jessica said nothing, but her posture had stiffened, and the jade eyes had gone cold as stone once more.

Beads of sweat broke out along my hairline and on the back of my neck. I couldn't say yes to this. There was no way I could handle being around Jessica on a regular basis—I'd proved that to myself years ago.

"I wish I could, man—truly," I told Hap. "But this is a surprise, and I'm already fully committed elsewhere. I tell you what—I'll pull my best guy from a detail he was supposed to start tomorrow and put him on it. Anthony and I ran missions together in Afghanistan and Iraq, and you couldn't ask for anyone more qualified and reliable."

Hap didn't look thrilled, but he let out a breath and gave me a resigned nod. "I guess that'll have to do. I can't lie though —I'm disappointed."

I tried not to cringe. I hated letting Hap down. But better my friend be disappointed with me than murder me.

Like most older brothers, Hap had always been protective of Jessica. Back in high school, he'd fiercely warned all his friends she was off-limits, me included.

Especially me. Back then I'd tried my very best to live up to the first syllable in my name, enjoying all the perks that had come with being a star athlete and high school hero.

But the shy, artsy girl had always drawn my notice. Having no sisters of my own, I'd found her extreme femininity a source of fascination since the first day I'd met her. Later, it was her sharp sense of humor and the song lyrics she wrote. They were nothing short of poetry.

Most of all it had been her sweet voice that had done me in. She'd been a talented singer even then.

She was always humming something, and when she'd practiced in her room singing along with her guitar, the sound had drawn me like a magnet.

I'd made up excuses to hear her, claiming to be headed to the bathroom or to the kitchen for a snack when I really went to stand outside her door and listen. *That* ill-advised habit had led to one of the biggest mistakes of my life, and I wasn't taking any chances it would be repeated.

Turning my attention to Jessica, I apologized to her as well. "I'm sorry. I wish I wasn't so—"

She cut me off, her words curt. "Busy. I know. It's fine. It makes no difference to me. As you said, Anthony is qualified and reliable. I'm looking forward to meeting him tomorrow. Thanks for stopping by, Wilder. I'm sure I'll see you around."

She stood. "Hap—I'm going to go help Rachel clean up the breakfast dishes." And then she walked away, leaving Hap and me alone.

"She seems annoyed," I said.

"She's just tired. We all got to bed late because of the police situation, and she's been traveling non-stop for two years," Hap explained. "Also, I kind of sprang this on her. She wanted to brush off last night as no big deal and stick with her current security company. Ten bucks says she's going to accuse me of being a know-it-all bully as soon as you leave."

"She always did hate being told what to do," I mused, remembering the spats I'd witnessed between the brother and sister long ago.

"Yeah, she's changed in a lot of ways, but that's not one of them," Hap said, and now I was wondering exactly *how* Jessica had changed over the years.

Not your business. You'll never find out, and you shouldn't even wonder. Stick to security and don't let it get personal.

Out loud I said, "Well, we'll stay out of her way as much as possible. Like I said, Gray and I will go by on Tuesday and do a thorough eval. Anthony will be here tomorrow to escort her home and anywhere else she'd like to go while she's in Rhode Island. If she needs someone for personal protection on a more permanent basis, I can start looking into that."

"Thanks man. I do appreciate it. I'd better not make any more decisions for her if I know what's good for me."

Hap laughed and slapped my back as we started toward the front door. "I already feel better, though, knowing you're involved. There's no one in the world I trust more than you with my little sister."

I swallowed hard against a sudden guilty lump in my throat as I accepted my friend's handshake. "I won't let you down."

"I know you won't."

Leaving the mansion, I was agitated and restless and feeling a bit like I'd dodged a bullet with my name engraved on it.

I had a full schedule today, which was good. I loved being busy. Busy left very little time for thinking. About Jessica—and *other* troubling aspects of my past.

As I frequently told my buddies, distraction was a man's best friend. Speaking of that, before pulling my car out of Hap's drive, I picked up my phone and tapped it to return a missed call.

It had come from an actress I spent time with occasionally. I suspected she might be a little more invested in the "friendship" than I was—we didn't have all that much in common as far as I could tell. But she was beautiful and fun, and she was in town for a few weeks between projects.

Maybe I should give it a chance? If I couldn't have the one I wanted, maybe I should try wanting the one who wanted *me*.

She picked up, and I forced myself to smile. "Bree—hey, sorry I missed your call. How are you?" I paused to listen to her answer before continuing. "Great. Listen, what are you up to tonight? Want to get together?"

We made plans, and I hung up, feeling marginally better. I had a few days to get my head straight before seeing Jessica again.

And I'd do whatever it took, filling every minute with work, play, and above all… distraction.

FOUR

Jessica

I moved around the guest room, gathering my things and stuffing them into my luggage with more force than was probably necessary.

When was I going to get over it? When was I going to finally move past this ridiculous and futile crush on Wilder Lowe?

Maybe it was because he was my first kiss, maybe it was the way he used to compliment my songwriting and take my dreams seriously all those years ago, but I seemed to have zero control over my reaction to him.

Frankly it was becoming pathetic.

The man couldn't be less interested. In fact, I was surprised he'd even bothered to come by and meet with me today.

He'd practically yawned his way through the conversation and done everything in his power to limit his involvement.

If not for his friendship with Hap, he could probably have cared less *what* happened to me. Well, I wasn't a charity case, and I didn't need him—or my over-protective, overbearing brother—to take care of me.

Jamming my sleep t-shirt into my overnight bag, I zipped it and headed for the bedroom door, dragging my larger suitcase behind me.

At the bottom of the stairs, Hap spotted me.

"What are you doing? Where are you going?"

"Home."

"Now? Why?"

"I want to get settled. I want to unpack and relax, and I've got a new song idea I want to work on. My piano is there."

"But your bodyguard can't start until tomorrow," Hap argued.

I stopped and turned to face him. "I changed my mind about that. It's silly to have Wilder pull the guy off a detail he's already scheduled for him. Nothing actually happened last night. Nothing's *ever* happened here at my Eastport Bay house except for a wind gust—it's perfectly safe."

Hap started to argue. "But—"

I held up a hand. "I've already called my security company and asked them to send an extra guard today—he'll probably be there by the time I reach the house. I appreciate what you were trying to do this morning, but I really can take care of myself."

Reading his unhappy expression, my heart softened. "If it'll make you feel better, I'll meet Anthony tomorrow, and I'll let him follow me around whenever I go somewhere that crowd control is an issue. But this is my hometown, Hap. I want to be just a regular person here and go to the grocery store and CVS and Nooky's diner for pancakes without an entourage. You know how it is, don't you?"

Hap nodded. "I get it. But you're more famous than I ever was. I'm not sure it's possible for you. People recognize you *everywhere.*"

"Well, I'm not going out today or tonight anyway. I'm just going to unpack and work on my song, maybe take a bath and have ice cream for dinner and settle in for a Netflix binge. I just want to be *home*."

After a long moment of silence, Hap let out a sigh. "Okay. Well, if you can wait ten minutes, I'll drop you off on my way into work. We're editing the season finale of Tech House, and I was just about to go in. Let me grab my coffee and my keys and say good-bye to Rachel. I assume you've already told her?"

I smiled. "Yes, and she agrees with me. I'll go put my bags in your car."

Hap shook his head, grabbing the larger one. "I'll get this one. See you in a minute."

As we arrived at my house, I rolled down the Lamborghini's passenger side window and spoke to the guard at the gatehouse. He'd met my brother before, but it had been a while.

"Hi Doug."

"Hey Miss Bailey. It's good to see you. Welcome home."

"Thanks. It's good to *be* home—finally. You remember my brother Hap?"

The two men exchanged greetings, and Doug opened the gate for us. Hap pulled forward into the driveway, stopping the car as close to my front door as possible.

He got out and dragged my heavy bag from the back seat. Once we were inside, Hap set the suitcase down and pulled out his phone.

"I want you to call me or Rachel if you need anything. I'll be working late tonight, but I know she'd be thrilled to hang out with you if you change your mind or get lonely."

He tapped on the screen. "And I'm texting you Wilder's number, in case you change your mind about having him come by with Gray and check out the house."

"You don't have to do that," I started to protest, but my phone beeped with an incoming text notification.

Hap's unrepentant grin displayed the dimples that had made his childhood face instantly recognizable and adored by television viewers nationwide.

"Too late. Love you, Kermit."

I stretched up to hug him goodbye. "Love you too, bossy big brother. I'll talk to you soon."

* * *

It was nice to be home—at first.

It felt good to sit down at my own familiar piano—the same one I'd learned to play on—and mess around with the beginnings of a new song. It was nice to walk around in my old super-soft fleece pants and a ratty flannel shirt, eating ice cream straight from the carton and not even worrying when some splotched onto my fuzzy socks.

I chuckled to myself. *If my fans could see "glamorous" Jade now.*

After throwing the socks into the washer along with the clothes from my suitcase, I soaked in a hot bath until my fingers pruned. Then I snuggled under the covers and streamed an entire season of a show I'd heard people talking about but hadn't had time to watch while on tour.

When it was over, I was left with a bit of a hollow feeling inside. It wasn't that the show hadn't ended well—it was actually really good.

It was just there was no one *there* to discuss it with.

I texted with my makeup artist Serena, who'd recommended the series to me. Then I scrolled my feeds for a while, responding to some kind fan comments and posting a picture from backstage at Gillette Stadium with me and all the members of my tour.

I thanked them and all my fans for an incredible two-year

run and told them I was taking a little social media hiatus to rest and recuperate.

There was a flurry of responses, which was sweet. But again... those people weren't *here*. No one was.

Suddenly the house seemed exceptionally quiet—and way too big for one person to live in alone. Maybe I'd sell it and get something a little cozier.

Before turning in for the night, I checked in with Hugh, the new night watchman who'd been sent over today from my security company.

"I'm getting ready to go to bed. Everything good?"

"Yes ma'am, Miss Bailey. All quiet."

"Okay thanks. I'll probably sleep in, so I may not see you until tomorrow night."

"Yes ma'am. Sleep well."

A deafening wail woke me from a dream where I was swimming in my ocean-facing pool—with Wilder Lowe of all people.

Sitting straight up in bed, I blinked a few times and looked around the dark room, wondering what the sound was, *where* I was, and whether I might still be dreaming.

My body clock still out of whack from travel, I'd taken a melatonin tablet before bed. It had worked a little *too* well—my head felt swimmy and slow.

It cleared abruptly when the sound finally registered. It was an alarm. A security alarm.

My heart left its usual position and slammed up into my throat.

I was home in Eastport Bay, and the piercing noise was signaling a breach of one of the doors or windows.

Or a gust of wind. That was all it had been last night. But still, I was taking no chances. I reached for my phone to dial 9-1-1.

The alarm stopped.

The silence in its wake was almost surreal. I set the phone back down. It must have been another false alarm and my security guards had turned it off.

Still, I wasn't likely to go right back to sleep after that. My heart was still pounding, and my hands were trembling to the point the phone rattled as I set it back on my nightstand.

Leaving my room, I padded down the wood-floored hallway on bare feet, intending to locate one of the guards and make sure everything was okay.

There was no sound from downstairs, no conversation or sound of shoes on marble.

When I reached the top of the staircase, I realized I was naked—I usually slept that way. Probably not the best look for a chat with my security personnel.

Instead of going down, I peered over the balcony railing to the first floor, intending to call out to Hugh and verbally confirm that things were okay.

The words froze in my throat as I spotted a shadow moving below.

Squinting into the darkness, I tried to make it out. It looked like someone was moving silently through the foyer, heading for the base of the staircase.

Could it be Hugh? It was definitely a man, but I couldn't see his face.

Either he had black hair, or wore a dark knit cap. And I was pretty sure he wasn't wearing a security staff uniform.

Clad all in black, he was dressed more like... a burglar.

For a half-second, I was frozen in terror. Then my heart started beating again—well in excess of its normal pace.

The sound of it roared in my ears, preventing me from hearing anything else—footsteps on the staircase, for instance.

I wasn't going to stick around for visual confirmation that an intruder was in my house and coming for me. I turned and ran back to my room, shutting the door behind me—quietly I hoped—and locked it.

Grabbing my phone from the nightstand first, I ran into the attached bathroom.

After locking the bathroom door, I flipped off the light switch and headed for the large walk-in closet, closing myself inside.

That's where I finally stopped and sank to the carpeted floor, crouching behind the large square shape of the shoe tower that centered the closet.

It took me four tries to successfully dial 9-1-1. My hands were shaking so hard I kept hitting the wrong keys.

"Nine-one-one what's your emergency?"

"I think there's been a break-in at my house," I answered in a strangled whisper, reluctant to speak too loudly in case the intruder was now upstairs and searching for me.

Maybe he *wasn't* looking for me. Maybe all he wanted was valuables. He could have them, as long as he left me alone.

"You'll have to speak up please. I can't hear you," the operator said.

I spoke a little louder. "There's someone in my house. Please send the police."

The operator asked for my address then commented, "We just had a patrol out there last night for a false alarm."

"Well this is a *real* one," I hissed. "I saw someone in my house."

"You're there alone?"

"No. There are two security guards here, too, but I don't know where they are."

"Are you sure it wasn't one of them you saw?" the operator asked.

"Yes. I don't know. I don't think so." The woman had me questioning myself. "Please just send someone. I'm afraid."

"Alright, they're on their way, ma'am. I'm going to put you on hold, but I'll be right back—"

I hung up and dialed Hap. There was no way I was going to just sit in my closet waiting for the emergency operator—who may or may not have thought I was crazy. If these were my last few minutes of life, I wanted to spend them talking to someone I loved.

After several unanswered rings, I remembered Hap saying he'd be working late tonight. He must not have had his phone near him or had silenced it while he worked. Or maybe he had headphones on while editing.

Holding the phone to my chest, I strained my ears for any indication of approaching sirens or sounds outside the closet door.

Had the intruder managed to unlock my bedroom and bathroom doors?

By now he could be standing right there outside the closet, about to come in and do God knows what to me. This could be it for me—the end.

Well, I wasn't going to make it easy for him. Looking around, I grabbed a black patent stiletto shoe. It was the closest thing I could find to a weapon. They certainly hurt my feet enough.

Where *were* my security guards? How could an intruder have gotten past the watchman at the gate and the two of them at the house?

Hap had been right—that company was *so* fired. That was if I lived long enough to fire them.

Why hadn't I listened to him and waited another day to come home? If I had, the bodyguard from Wilder's firm would have been here with me, and I'd be safe.

Wilder.

Swiping my phone again to wake it, I brought up Hap's last text and tapped the number he'd sent me.

Though it was the middle of the night, Wilder answered on the first ring, a sleepy rasp softening his deep voice. "Hello?"

"Wilder? It's me, Jessica."

His tone crackled with sudden alertness. "Jessica, are you okay? What's going on? Are you with Hap?"

"No. I'm at home alone, and I'm scared. I think there's someone in my house. The alarm went off and then stopped."

Unlike the emergency operator, Wilder didn't question my instincts. "I'll be there in two minutes. Where in the house are you? Are you somewhere safe?"

"I hope so. I locked the bedroom door and the bathroom, and I'm in my closet. It's upstairs, the third door on the—"

He broke in. "I know where it is. I looked at the blueprints and floorplan of your house this morning. Stay there and be quiet. Don't open the door for anyone but me, okay?"

I nodded rapidly, then realizing I hadn't actually said anything, issued a breathy, "Okay."

"Good girl. You did exactly the right thing. Everything's gonna be okay."

"Hurry Wilder."

"I will hummingbird. I'll be there before you know it. You hang tight."

My call-waiting notification beeped. "Nine-one-one is calling me back," I told Wilder.

"Okay, answer it. They might be telling you that officers are at your door, but don't leave the closet, you hear me? Just tell them you're all right and you're hiding—they'll find a way inside."

He paused before adding, "And mention to them I'm on my way, so they don't shoot me. I'm less than a minute away now."

FIVE

The Dangerous Kind of Danger

Wilder

I threw my car into park at the curb outside the gatehouse at Jessica's estate.

There were no police cars on the scene yet. The guard there recognized me from the previous day when I'd stopped by to check out the grounds and the home's exterior security measures.

"Hey Mr. Lowe. Whatcha doing back here?"

In his mid-to-late twenties with a soft, kind-looking face, he was about as intimidating as a fuzzy bathrobe. He certainly seemed relaxed and unconcerned. He was literally eating a donut.

Had the security staff already checked out the alarm and cleared the scene then?

"The security alarm went off, I said. "Didn't you hear it?"

"Oh yeah, I heard it, but it stopped after a minute. I thought it was another false alarm like yesterday. Anyway, I figured the other two guys were handling it."

I could barely contain my contempt as I rushed past him—I had no time to waste on this incompetent man.

Amateur hour. "Thanks a lot."

"No problem." He gave me a wave and took another large bite of his pastry.

Once inside the gate, I ran down the drive and to the front of the house, checking the door for forced entry. It was closed and locked.

I turned and ran toward the rear of the home—that was the most likely point of entry. As I went, I took stock of the seaside mansion's generous windows, noting that each one I passed seemed to be closed tight.

When I reached the back terrace, there was no more mystery about what had triggered the security alarm. The back door had clearly been tampered with.

My flashlight picked up on the shiny metal edges of fresh nicks around the keyhole, an indication of lock bumping.

Before going inside, I opened my gear bag and withdrew a helmet outfitted with special four-tube night-vision goggles. We'd used similar gear during my SEAL days, and I made sure my entire team at Viridian had access to the pricey but highly modified equipment.

The helmet-mounted goggles gave me the ability to see in complete darkness and would allow me the element of surprise should the intruder still be inside Jessica's house.

The idea of a strange man in the house with her caused my heart to thump a couple of extra beats.

When she'd called and I'd heard the terror in her voice, it had stopped altogether. Then I'd sprung into action, driving like a Formula One racer through the deserted streets of Eastport Bay to get here, my mind working overtime as the precious seconds ticked by.

I was no stranger to high pressure situations—I was built for them. While many people became paralyzed by fear, the threat of danger caused all of my senses to shift into a heightened state, my adrenaline pumping until I felt capable of superhuman feats.

But this wasn't war. I didn't even know if there *was* an enemy on the premises. All I knew was that Jessica was afraid, and I had to get to her.

Putting on the helmet and drawing the gun from my shoulder holster, I slipped inside the open door and moved cautiously through the house toward the staircase.

At first I saw no one—then the shape of a prone body came into view. Off to one side of the curved staircase landing, a uniformed man lay unconscious.

Or dead.

I stole over to him and felt for a pulse. Locating one and determining the man was breathing, I moved forward toward the bottom step. I'd make sure the guy got medical attention later—right now, protecting Jessica was priority number one.

There was no more doubt an intruder had been in the house. The question now was whether he was *still* there—and if he'd gotten to Jessica.

My gut twisted in a sickening knot, and tension pounded in my temples. Listening and watching for any sign of movement, I crept up the stairs, gun cocked and ready.

At the top I found the hallway empty. I moved quickly to Jessica's bedroom door and tried the knob.

It was locked. Which meant one of two things—the intruder hadn't made it past this point, and Jessica was safe inside alone—or he *had* breached the bedroom door and was in there with her right now.

No time to wait.

Lifting a booted foot, I kicked the door open, did a quick scan of the room then moved to the closed and locked door of the master bath, repeating the maneuver. Closet doors didn't generally have locks, so I simply turned the knob and entered.

And was struck in the forehead by some sort of projectile as a fierce shriek ripped the silence.

Flipping the light switch, I spotted the object that had struck me just above the right eyebrow and come within inches of blinding me—a high-heeled shoe with a *very* pointy stiletto heel.

I scanned the rest of the closet's interior and spotted Jessica. She was crouched in the farthest corner, furled into a ball of limbs and long, sleep-mussed hair.

"Good thing you didn't have a knife. I'd be dead. That's a mean throwing arm you've got there, kiddo."

"Oh Wilder—it's you!"

There was a flurry of motion as Jessica burst from the corner and flung herself at me. Reacting on instinct, I wrapped my arms around her, stroking her hair and back in a soothing motion as I murmured.

"I'm here. You're okay. You're safe."

Her entire body was trembling, and something deep inside me cracked. Pure emotion leaked from the fissure. Relief. Joy. Fierce devotion.

That last one was trouble. Emotion plus Jessica equaled danger—*not* the good kind of danger that got my adrenaline going and pumped me for a fight—the *dangerous* kind of danger that had long-lasting, friendship-ending consequences.

Wrapping my fingers around her upper arms, I set Jessica away from me, ran my gaze down her body then quickly back up again when I realized she was completely nude.

I kept my eyes trained on her wide, frightened ones.

"Why are you naked?"

"What?" She glanced down at herself. "Oh."

Grabbing the garment hanging immediately to her right, she yanked it from the hanger and clutched it to the front of her body, almost—but not quite—concealing her nudity. It was a sparkly hot-pink evening gown.

Only Jessica Bailey could manage to look glamorous and sexy during a home invasion.

"Did you see him?" she asked in a high, shaky voice.

I shook my head, choosing not to tell her about the unconscious guard at the moment. She was already so shaken.

"No."

"Was it another false alarm?"

"No. I'm afraid it wasn't. Someone was here. I think I might have scared him away."

"How do you know someone was here then?"

I couldn't lie to her. "I saw one of your guards unconscious downstairs. He'd been either knocked out or drugged—I didn't spend enough time with him to determine which. I was in a hurry to get to you."

I tilted her chin up with one finger, so her eyes were forced to meet mine. "Are you okay?"

Jessica looked like she might be in shock. Her pupils were enlarged, and her skin was ashen. Finally, she nodded and murmured a quiet, "Yeah. I think so."

Hearing sirens, I led her out of the closet through the bathroom to her bedroom where I rummaged through her drawers.

"What are you looking for?" she asked.

"A sweatshirt and some pants. And some underwear. For you. I thought you might be..." My eyes went to her bare shoulders and hips and long, toned legs, which were still exposed. "...cold."

Jessica blinked, looking down again. She appeared to be emerging from her state of shock. "Right. Yes. I should put something on before the police arrive."

Too late. A pair of officers charged into the bedroom, weapons drawn. I immediately held both my hands out to the side.

Unfortunately, a pair of silky pink panties hung from my pinky finger.

Great. Now they're going to think I'm a pervert who broke in to raid her panty drawer. Or worse.

Jessica was naked except for the evening gown that covered her breasts and a strip of skin down the middle of her body.

I could really be in trouble here.

Speaking slowly and clearly, I said, "I'm Wilder Lowe with Veridian Security. I'm carrying a Sig Sauer P229 semi-automatic pistol—it's in a shoulder holster under my left arm. I'm her security."

It wasn't *technically* true—not yet—but it was about to be. There was no way I'd stand by and let her current company bungle things yet again.

Tonight's mistake could have been deadly. I didn't want to think what could have happened to Jessica if I hadn't arrived when I did.

"Is that true ma'am?" one of the officers asked, giving the pink panties an evil eye.

Jessica nodded rapidly. "Yes. I called him. I asked him to come."

Lowering their weapons, both officers approached her. The female one asked, "Are you hurt?"

"No. Just shook up. Someone was in the house."

The older male officer checked out her bedroom door, which was hanging off its hinges. "Did the perpetrator get to you?"

I raised a hand. "Um, that was me." Shooting Jessica a sheepish grin, I added, "I kind of messed up your doors. I'll pay for the damage."

"Don't be silly. You were trying to protect me." She turned her attention to the police officers. "Did you find anything? See anyone?"

"We found a security guard outside, unconscious. He's

alive but he appears to have been drugged. There was a coffee cup on the ground near him. We're going to have it analyzed," the woman said.

"There's another guard downstairs, passed out. We called an ambulance for them. You sure you don't want to go to the hospital?" the male officer asked.

Jessica shook her head. "No. I'm fine. Can you tell if it was a burglary? Did it look like the downstairs had been ransacked or anything?"

"Not that I saw. From the looks of it, your backdoor lock was picked," the man said. "We'll do a thorough search of the property for any additional evidence. Do you feel well enough to stay around for a while and help us determine if anything was taken?"

"Sure. Of course."

"If you don't mind, I'd like to stay as well," I said. "I want to find out what we're dealing with—in case burglary *wasn't* the motive."

The officers agreed, and I walked over to Jessica, pressing the panties into her hand. "Get dressed then we'll do a room-by-room inventory. First, give Hap and Rachel a call to let them know what's going on."

I wanted assurances her brother and sister-in-law would be on hand to see to her emotional needs while I did the work of figuring out just what the hell this home invader was after.

I hoped it *was* just material things—which could be replaced—and not Jessica, who most certainly could not.

After clearing the upstairs and determining nothing had been taken, we all went downstairs. That's when I saw it.

Taking Jessica's arm, I turned her toward the kitchen. "Want some water or something? You should probably have some."

Hopefully she hadn't seen it too.

The coil of paracord—sometimes used to bind or choke

victims—lying near the spot where the unconscious security guard had lain at the base of the stairs. There was also a digital camera.

I exchanged a significant glance with one of the officers before guiding Jessica away from the disturbing sight. I'd tell her about it eventually, but for right now I didn't want her to be any more frightened than necessary.

After a few minutes, the female officer joined us in the kitchen. She was holding the camera in her gloved hands.

"Miss Bailey, would you mind taking a look at this?"

"At what?"

The officer held out the camera with its display screen facing Jessica. "Do you recognize anything in these photos? It looks like some of them might have been taken inside the house."

While I watched from over Jessica's shoulder, the officer scrolled through the camera's photo inventory with a gloved fingertip. I heard Jessica's breath fracture.

"Yes. That's my home gym. And the last one was the sunroom. But these were taken during the daytime." Glancing up at the officer she asked, "What does that mean? Was he in the house already when I got here today?"

"He could have been here on a previous day, casing the place," the woman suggested. "It looks like he is a cat burglar, because the other photos are from different houses."

She stopped scrolling and dropped the camera to her side.

Jessica let out a gasp, reaching for the device. "Wait—let me see it again. Go back."

Her body started quaking so hard I could feel it from my stance behind her. Her voice shook as well.

"That's... that's my house in Malibu. And that one's from my place in Aspen. These are all from *inside* my houses. Oh my God, this one's from my apartment in Manhattan. It has a twenty-four-hour doorman and needs a special elevator key to access. How did he get these? When was he *inside* all my houses?"

Now she turned her head and looked up at me, her green eyes wide with panic. "Wilder?"

Obviously she expected me to have some answers. I didn't. But I was sure as fuck going to get some.

I turned her to face me and gripped her shoulders lightly. "Don't worry. We'll find out, and we're going to get this guy. I know people in each of those places, and I'll get someone on it right away."

"But how does he know so much about me? What is he doing in my homes? What does he want?" Her voice seemed to go up an octave with each successive question.

I cupped one of her cheeks in my hand. "I don't know, hummingbird. We'll figure it out. And in the meantime, I don't want you to worry. You're going to be safe."

"How can you say that?" she asked. "How do you know?"

"Because my firm is taking over your security."

SIX

My Own Personal Hell

Wilder

With all the celebrity clients I dealt with, I'd seen numerous stalker cases, and I knew the difference between a minor threat and a major one.

This guy was off the charts.

After Jessica had left with Hap and Rachel—with a two-man detail I'd assigned to protect them until I joined them myself for the night—I went through the rest of the camera's contents with the police detectives.

There were more interior shots of Jessica's properties. But that wasn't the worst of it.

The one that chilled me to the bone was a selfie of the stalker in Jessica's bed with his head resting on her pillow.

A blanket covered his face, but a few strands of blond hair peeked out. On the pillow next to him was an enlarged photo of Jessica's face from a spread in Vanity Fair.

"This is weird," the newly arrived detective said. "Some kind of fantasy role-play? But it could be helpful. I can't believe he left it behind."

I nodded in agreement. "It's definitely a lucky break. I must have surprised him by entering the house. My guess is that he'd set these things down while dealing with the security guard in the foyer."

"Maybe he dropped them in the struggle?"

"I didn't see any signs of a struggle. I'll bet toxicology will find Rohypnol in those coffee cups."

"You think the rope was for the guard too?"

I matched the officer's grim expression. "No. I don't."

"Yeah, me either."

"From the looks of those photos, he's been getting bolder and bolder, working his way toward a bigger event," I said. "I think he's been amping himself up to take her—and that he'd decided last night was the night."

"Any thoughts on who it could be?" the detective asked.

"No, I just took over her security today. My people are speaking with her former company to see if they have any likely suspects. In the meantime, I'm going to send her somewhere safe with my best guy."

"Where's safe? This stalker seems to have a bead on all her movements."

"That's why she's going to make an unexpected one," I said.

* * *

Fifteen minutes later, I was standing outside the door of Gray Lupine's townhouse in Eastport Bay's Harbor district.

The briny smell of ocean air soothed my agitated senses but did nothing to lessen my impatience.

I raised my hand to knock again just as Gray yanked open the door.

"What is it? What's happening?" My buddy's usually neat

hair was in disarray, sticking up all over his head. He wore only a pair of long shorts, his dark eyes bleary.

Without a shirt, the network of tattoos stretching across his chest and shoulders was visible in the low lamplight. He'd gotten in late from a gig on the West Coast and had probably only gone to bed an hour or two earlier.

"Can I come in?"

"Of course. I love company at four-thirty a.m." Gray said in a surly tone. "Feels like the good old days. Are we gonna pay a surprise visit to the Taliban or something?"

"No but you *are* gonna have to get dressed and pack—you're going away for a while."

"What? Where? I thought you wanted me on the Hood project. You said it was priority number one."

"Yeah, well there's a new priority. Jessica Bailey was nearly abducted tonight, and you're going to get her out of town and stay with her until we find the guy who's after her."

All traces of grogginess cleared from Gray's eyes. "The pop star? You serious?"

"Always am. He broke into her house on Atlantic Avenue tonight—had roofies, rope, and a camera—the works. I'm pretty sure he was still there when I got there, but he slipped away."

Gray whistled. "Wow. What alerted you? An alarm? I thought she turned down the deal to take over her security."

"She did. She called me when the alarm went off."

Gray gave me a funny look but only said, "I see."

I carried on, all business. "I spoke to the pilot. It's wheels up at nine a.m. so you're gonna need to pack fast and then meet with Frasier to go over the Hood project details. He'll be taking over while you're gone."

"Okay if that's what you want," Gray said. Hesitating a beat, he continued. "Can I ask why you're sending *me* on this detail?"

"Because you're the best. I trust you more than anyone."

Gray's head bobbed up and down, but his tone was uncertain.

"Okaayyyy," he dragged the word out. "But you said I was the only one who could do the Hood project. And while I'd be delighted to 'guard the body' of a gorgeous pop star, my specialty is in home security, not personal security."

I frowned. "Well, who else would you suggest?"

"You," Gray said. "It's your area of expertise. And you usually take on the most high-profile clients."

"Well, I can't take this one."

"Why not?"

"It's just..." I shook my head. "...not a good idea. Believe me, in this case, I'm *not* the best man for the job."

Understanding dawned across Gray's face. "Oh I see... you've got a thing for this girl."

Biting my lip, I turned my head to the side and stared at a photo on the wall. "I wouldn't call it a 'thing.'"

"Well, what would you call it then?"

"Suffice it to say, this case is too... *personal* to me. I've known the girl practically all our lives. Her brother is my best friend. It's just not a good idea."

Gray studied me. "You're still hung up on that Iraq incident, aren't you? Man, you gotta let that go. There was nothing you could have done. None of us could have. That was the commander—not us—and nothing we can do will bring that girl back."

I swallowed hard, my throat suddenly feeling sore. "Yeah, but we were supposed to protect her. And she's dead."

"I know man, and that truly sucks. It took me a while to get over, too, but you gotta stop beating yourself up about it. You keep trying to prove something that's already been proved a thousand times over."

"I just can't let it happen again. Jessica is too important."

"And that's why you *are* the best man for the job," he said. "Who's going to care more than you do about her safety? One of the guys who's never even met her, who doesn't understand how important she is? Who sees her as just another spoiled, rich celebrity?"

Gray went on. "Listen, if you tell me to do it, I'll do it. I'll be on that plane. You know I'd do anything for you after all you've done for me. But I hate to see you running scared from things that shouldn't scare you. You can handle it. You can handle anything. You're the strongest person I know."

My lips rolled inward, and I looked at the ground. "Thanks man, I appreciate it. But I think this is the one thing I *can't* handle. I'm heading over to her brother's house to tell her what's going on. I'll call you in a bit with more details, okay?"

On the drive to Hap's house, I thought about my friend's words. *Was* I still hung up about the happenings in Iraq that had effectively ended my SEAL career?

I didn't think so. I'd made a great life for myself since then and was generally pretty content. My new career involved plenty of challenging assignments, and I'd protected a number of important clients in risky situations.

What Gray didn't understand—couldn't possibly understand—was just *how* important this one was.

And that the stalker wasn't the only threat facing Jessica. If I whisked her away to a private location where it was just the two of us...

No, I couldn't take the detail myself. Passing it on to my right-hand man was the best thing I could do for *everyone* involved.

Hap opened the door before I even got there. Clearly he wasn't sleeping tonight either. Or was it morning now? I checked my watch. Yeah—it was after five am. Sleep or no sleep, that qualified as morning.

"Did they catch him?" Hap asked as I stepped inside.

"No. How's Jessica?"

"She's sleeping. Rachel insisted she take a sleep aid because she was so wired. So what now? She can't go back to that house—not until he's caught."

"Definitely not. And I don't think she should go to any of her other homes either. I'm not sure if Jessica told you, but there was a camera left at the scene. The guy has been inside all her properties."

"I heard. How is that possible by the way?" Hap asked. "How could he know so much about her? And how did he know she was going to be in Eastport Bay last night? One of the detectives told me it looked like a kidnapping attempt."

I nodded grimly. "That's what I think, too."

"Shit." Hap shifted from one foot to the other, his hands flexing then folding into fists. He looked like he wanted to punch someone but didn't know who.

"The guy might have made an educated guess about last night since it was the end of her tour and her last show was in Boston," I said. "I'm not sure about all the other incidents. I'm guessing the Rhode Island State Police are going to coordinate with the other states and start trying to figure it out, but I'm not waiting for that. I'm going to pull a few strings and get some people working on it privately. In the meantime, the most important thing is keeping Jessica safe."

"How do you propose to do that?" Hap was pacing now.

"If the perp knows about her schedule and all her houses, he probably knows about this house, too, and the billionaire bachelor house—*and* our parents' house," he said, his voice rising in volume and pitch. "And she can't exactly go into witness protection or whatever. She's recognized all over the world. Even if she goes some place she's never been, someone will see her and snap a pic. It'll be online within five minutes, and he'll know where she is. A guy that obsessed is bound to turn up anywhere."

"I agree. Which is why until we find him, she's going to go where there's no one around to recognize her and post photos."

"Where?" Hap asked.

"A remote location I know of. It's very secure—completely off the grid. She could stay there for up to a year if necessary without ever having to leave for provisions. I sent someone over to her house to grab her suitcases and anything else they think she might need. Gray will meet her at the airport at nine to go with her."

"You're not going to tell me where?"

"It's best if the fewest people possible know the location. Right now, even Gray doesn't know where he's going. The pilot will set down in the region and they'll travel from there, so he won't know exactly where they are either. I'm the only one who knows about this place."

I set a reassuring hand on my friend's shoulder. "She'll be safe there—trust me."

Hap skewered me with a penetrating look. "I do trust you. *You.* Not Gray, not someone else. I don't know them. But I know you down to your soul. *You're* the one I want looking after my baby sister. Do this for me, man. I won't ask you for anything else ever again, but this is life and death. I need you. *She* needs you. Take care of her. Please."

Fuck. How was I supposed to say no to an ask like that? But how could I say yes?

As beautiful as the remote compound was, as much as I enjoyed spending time there, it *could* end up being an extended stay... just me and Jessica.

She was hard enough to resist at a distance. Weeks or months on a private island with her would be tantamount to my own personal hell.

Hap walked over to a chair in the entry hall where a woman's purse sat. Opening it, he drew out a wallet and extracted something from it. He carried the object back to me and held it out for me to see.

"Remember this? I spotted it last night when Jessica was checking to see how much cash she had on her."

I took the photo and studied it. It was of the three of us—Hap, Jessica, and me when we were younger. She stood between me and her brother, both our baby-faces turned toward whoever was taking the picture.

Jessica wasn't looking at the camera.

She was looking at me.

"She's always looked up to you," Hap said. "Like another big brother."

Inside, I cringed. I hoped nothing showed on the outside. I had *never* looked at Jessica like a sister and never could.

Hap went on, his eyes imploring. "She's known you practically her whole life. She trusts you completely. Please, Wild. Do this for me."

The combination of the look on Jessica's young face and the raw note in my friend's voice was the final straw. I nodded slowly.

"Can I keep this?" I asked, holding up the photo. "I was having a really good hair day."

The joke lightened Hap's troubled expression. "Sure. I'm sure she won't mind."

"Then yes. I'll do it."

Hap's breath rushed out in an audible whoosh, and he grabbed me in a fierce, brief hug. "Thank you. Thank you. I'll owe you one forever."

"You don't owe me anything." I pulled away. "I've got a few more things to take care of before we go. I need to run by my place and throw some clothes in a bag, grab my passport, call the pilot and Gray and let them know about the change in plans. Will you make sure she's ready to go by eight-thirty?"

"Absolutely. And I'll tell her the good news that you're her new bodyguard."

"I'm sure she'll be delighted," I quipped and headed for the door.

SEVEN
Sedate and Reliable

Jessica

I was furious.

Practically stomping up the boarding steps into the private jet, I stowed my carry-on under my seat and fell into the soft leather with a grunt.

The last thing I'd expected to hear this morning was that I'd be going on a trip—with Wilder. I mean, the guy could barely be bothered to *look* at me much less make conversation. This was going to be one awkward flight.

"Why can't you tell me where we're going?"

In the seat across from me, Wilder offered me a patient, if not pleasant, smile.

"Because to keep you completely secure, I need to make sure no one knows where we're going. I didn't even tell Hap."

"But I'm the one who's *going* there. It's not like I'll tell anyone."

"Can I see your phone please?" he extended his hand.

Baffled, I pulled the device from my purse and handed it to him. He started scrolling through my text messages.

"What the hell do you think you're doing?" I demanded.

"Did you call any of your friends last night? Did you text anyone and tell them what's going on?"

My face heated with embarrassment, like I was a seventh grader who'd been caught passing notes in class. "Well... I had to since you wouldn't let me check in on social media or anything. I was afraid they'd think I was dead. I also informed my agent and manager I'll be out of contact for a while."

Wilder sighed. "I'll need all their names, numbers, and addresses. Anyone else? Is there a significant other who's going to be trying to track you down and causing trouble when he can't?"

The flames beneath my skin burned even hotter. "No," I bit out. "Not at the moment."

"What happened to that hockey player?" He smirked. "Or was he just fodder for a new break-up song?"

Now I felt hot for a different reason. Anger. "We weren't a good fit. And no, I'm *not* writing a song about it."

The song was already finished, thank you very much, so technically, I wasn't writing it.

A pleased expression crossed Wilder's face, which somehow looked even more beautiful, in spite of the sleepless night. There was a bit of scruff on his chin and jawline, and his hair looked rumpled, as if he'd run his hands through it repeatedly over the past few hours.

He slid the back panel of my phone open and took out the battery, making a show of slipping it into his own pocket before returning the useless device to me.

He's mocking me, the gorgeous jerk.

"Do you really think I'd tell someone our top-secret destination? I realize this may come as a shock to you, but I'm not stupid. And I'm not some silly little pre-pubescent tween who can't wait to gossip to her friends. I've grown up, you know."

Wilder gave me a significant glance. "I'm well aware of that."

A wobbly sensation filled my mid-section. I counteracted it by doubling down on my annoyance.

"What are you even doing here?" I challenged. "I thought you were handing off the assignment to your right-hand man or something."

"I changed my mind."

"Why?"

There was a beat before he answered. "He reminded me I'd already put him in charge of another project, and no one else could handle it. It was his specialty."

"And what's your specialty."

"Personal protection."

"That means being a bodyguard, right?"

"Right, though I rarely take on details anymore."

"Why not?"

"I spend most of my time these days running the business."

"Who's going to do that while you're gone?"

He shrugged. "It'll be fine. Viridian Security will survive."

It didn't escape my notice that Wilder was giving me short, impersonal answers, as if I was a stranger asking him to share his deepest, darkest secrets without even buying him a drink first.

Oh yeah, this was going to be a *really* fun trip if all our conversations were as dry and stilted as this one. He was barely looking at me too, keeping his eyes down on the magazine he'd found onboard.

"You don't have to do this, you know. I could just stay with Hap and Rachel for a while with some extra security guards until they arrest this guy."

The jet began rolling down the runway, picking up speed

in preparation for takeoff. Wilder finally brought his gaze up to meet mine.

"Yes, I do. Believe me, I wouldn't be leaving behind my business and my life if it wasn't completely necessary."

Ouch. That stung. It was clear Wilder didn't want to be here. He'd never been interested in spending any time with me, and now he was being forced to. Probably by my big brother.

"Hap made you do this, didn't he? He guilt-tripped you into it."

Wilder deigned to hold eye contact with me a moment before answering. "He asked me to, yes."

"Well I don't need a babysitter," I snapped. "And I don't need your charity."

His lips twisted in a wry grin. "I'm being paid well enough. And even if I weren't, I don't need the money."

Obviously misreading the source of my irritation, he said, "Don't worry. They'll find the guy and put him away. You'll be back to your friends and boyfriends and your glamorous life soon enough. And I'm sure absence will only make the heart grow fonder where your adoring fans are concerned."

No doubt he was right about that last part. Absence certainly hadn't erased my feelings for Wilder. I was just as attracted to him as I'd been when we were teenagers, maybe even more so now that I was a woman, and he was a full-grown man.

"Look on the bright side," he said. "Maybe you can turn the experience into another hit song and gain even more fans—that is if you can survive the boredom of being alone with me for a week or two."

He laughed, the bright flash of his teeth against his tanned skin making my heart stutter and my brain fill with song lyrics about unrequited love.

No one had ever been *less* boring than this man. Or less available.

I woke as the plane descended, my ears popping from the change in altitude. We'd been flying for twenty-two hours.

Even from the air it was obvious we weren't in the United States anymore. The scenery outside the jet's windows looked tropical.

There were islands dotting a deep blue bay. A large modern-looking city came into view as we reached the mainland.

"Where are we?" I asked, sitting up and stretching.

"I'll tell you when we're off the plane," Wilder said. "I don't want to say anything until we're a good distance from any electronic equipment."

"You think the guy's been using my phone to track me or something? Is that why you removed the battery?"

"It's possible he could have hacked it. I don't want to take any chances of us being tracked, though we're not at our final destination yet. We've got a few hours still to go."

He stood and started gathering our luggage while the jet taxied toward a small, white stucco terminal building. Unzipping one of the bags, he withdrew a blonde wig, a pair of sunglasses with enormous round lenses, and a scarf.

"Here—put these on. And tug that scarf over your chin and mouth when we get off the plane—people will assume it's because of the air pollution."

Wilder donned a nondescript ballcap and sunglasses himself.

"I feel like we're about to walk through the airport in LA or something," I joked, but I put on the disguise.

We were definitely *not* in Los Angeles. Mangrove trees lined the runway, and the airport was surrounded by neighborhoods with narrow streets and smallish buildings with roofs of tin or Spanish tile.

When my appearance had been thoroughly altered, the jet's exit door opened, and we debarked. Wilder must have told the pilot to stay in the cockpit until we were gone because I never saw him.

Walking across the tarmac with Wilder, I asked, "Did the pilot know who was back there with you?"

"I told him I'd be accompanied by an unidentified female passenger." He grinned at me.

I grinned back. "That happen often?"

"Never."

A rush of pleasure filled me, though I wasn't sure if it was from his answer or that dazzling smile.

"So what now?" I asked.

"Now... we grab a cab to a car lot, buy a used Jeep or something, and take a drive."

"We're *buying* a car? No rental places here?" I guessed.

"There are, but I don't want to leave a trail. That's why I chose this private airport instead of the larger international one in the city. I'll be paying for the car—and anything else we need—in cash."

"Ah." I nodded. "By the way, I'm going to reimburse you for that and for the fuel for the plane and whatever else comes up."

"That's not necessary. These are business expenses."

"Well, you shouldn't have to pay them. And honestly, I have more money than I could ever spend," I said.

"Seems like you're finding a few ways to spend it. I didn't realize you had four houses."

A blush heated my neck and face, crawling toward my forehead as we walked in the sticky heat toward the cab line. "I like the ocean. And the mountains. And the city."

Wilder opened the back door of a cab and waited for me to slide in before getting in himself. He spoke in a language I didn't recognize, giving instructions to the driver, then settled back into the seat.

"I was just teasing," he said. "Believe me, when it comes to conspicuous consumption, I've seen it all. You're positively frugal compared to some of the clients I've had."

I laughed. "Do tell."

"I can't. Confidentiality agreement." He pulled his fingers across his closed lips, miming a zipper.

"Right. Wow, I guess the Wild-man really has become sedate and reliable."

A warm breeze blew through the open window as the cab drove through city streets lined with shops and restaurants, high rise hotels and palm trees.

The traffic was horrendous, the roads clogged with compact cars, motorcycles, and buses, so the going was slow. The people I saw were of such diverse skin tones and dress it was impossible for me to even guess which continent we were on.

"I was never *that* wild," Wilder argued, looking like *he* was blushing now.

"Well, you weren't *tame.* I was positively scandalized by some of the stories Hap told about you."

Wilder didn't respond, averting his eyes and training them on the windshield, watching the car's progress through the city streets where we passed a massive shopping mall and a tall, narrow monument surrounded by a park before moving into another dense business zone.

We stopped at a sketchy-looking used car dealership on the outer edges of the city. Wilder got out, instructing me to wait in the cab with the bags and speak to no one while he negotiated a "deal."

Ten minutes later he was paying the cabbie then helping me to climb into the front seat of a tired-looking older model SUV.

"You didn't tell me we'd be traveling in such luxury," I joked.

He shot me a grin. "No one's gonna take a second look at us traveling in this, which is good. Unfortunately, things are gonna get a bit worse before they get better."

"What does that mean?"

EIGHT
Off the Grid

Jessica

I discovered the answer on the five-hour drive that followed.

Our mysterious journey took us south out of the sprawling concrete jungle and across the countryside. Based on the people I saw walking on the roadside, riding bicycles, and driving in other cars, we were in an Asian country.

We traveled through tiny villages, which was nice, and on a winding mountain road which was not so nice.

It appeared to be a single lane in some spots—until other vehicles rounded the corner from the opposite direction and somehow passed by while we seemed to dangle from the edge of a cliff.

I found myself literally leaning toward the mountain, fearing my body weight alone would be enough to make us topple off the edge and crash into the ravine below.

"*This* is your idea of keeping me safe?" I asked during one particularly terrifying blind turn.

Wilder's white teeth flashed. "Don't worry. I know what

I'm doing. I've driven this road dozens of times. And the other drivers are native to the area."

"How do you know?"

"No one comes here who isn't a local—except for me."

Our cross-country trek ended at a small village perched on a beautiful remote stretch of coastline. Wilder drove down its main road then parked the SUV behind a row of low-slung buildings with thatched roofs.

"Are we there? Is this where we're staying?" I had zero doubt *no one* would ever look for me in a place like this. I wondered if it even appeared on the map.

"Just another pitstop," Wilder said. "I'm going to sell the SUV for parts. Just wait here—keep your sunglasses and scarf on. I'll be right back."

Within fifteen minutes, Wilder returned to the vehicle and began pulling the bags out of the back. "Okay, let's go. We're going to walk to the beach—it's close—just past these huts."

The beach was long and wide and very natural—not a lifeguard tower or bathhouse in sight.

Not far offshore, several small fishing boats were anchored alongside a surprisingly new-and-expensive-looking Sunseeker Predator yacht. I had been on boats like it before.

Small but luxurious, they typically had a large sunbathing area, a living area, and a dining area with wet bar, grill, and refrigerator on the upper deck.

Below deck would typically be a galley kitchen, a small breakfast seating area, a guest bathroom, and three private cabins, including a master bedroom with a much larger, posher bathroom en suite.

Wilder and I carried our bags right up to the edge of the water and watched as a local man swam out to one of the small boats. He unmoored it and motored it right up into the shallows so we could board.

"Did you buy this, too, or did you rent it?" I asked Wilder as we shuttled out to the beautiful yacht.

"Already owned it. Got it a couple years ago," Wilder explained.

I looked around at the distinctly un-cosmopolitan area. "And you keep it *here*?"

"Sometimes. I've taken it all over the world. It's a stroke of luck that it happened to be here now." Wilder climbed up to its rear deck and bent down, extending a hand. "Welcome aboard."

Once we were away from the beach and in open water, I asked, "*Now* can you tell me where we're going? Or at least where we are? I don't even know what ocean I'm on."

"It's the South China Sea. We're in Indonesia. The plane landed in Jakarta, and we drove to the southwest coast. That village back there is Bagedur. Now we're going to an island in the waters between Indonesia and Vietnam."

"An island? Which one?"

"It doesn't have a name. It's a private island," he said. "Indonesia is comprised of around eighteen thousand islands. Lots of the smaller ones are unnamed. Only six thousand of them are even inhabited."

"Wow. I didn't know that. And who inhabits this one?"

"For the next few days or weeks... we do."

"Just us?" I asked.

"Just us."

At the thought of spending several weeks alone on an island with Wilder, my stomach did a little flip. He was clearly less excited by the prospect than I was, if his grim expression was any indication.

I stopped asking questions and stayed quiet for the rest of the boat trip.

Last night's broken sleep aboard the jet was catching up

with me, and I napped out on the white-cushioned sundeck, lulled by the warm sun and cool breeze and the steady rhythm of the yacht as it cut through the ocean.

When I felt the boat slowing, I sat up and looked around. We were idling toward a wooden dock off to one side of a blinding white beach. A path led away from it into lush jungle foliage. Uphill from the beach, over the tops of the green tropical trees, loomed the roof of a large modern-looking structure.

I pointed to it. "Is that a house?"

"It is. The only one on the island."

"This is beautiful," I said, taking in the beach and the clear turquoise bay surrounding it. The scene was like a postcard. It seemed impossible a beach this idyllic was the playground of a sole resident.

"Wait till you see the view from up there." Wilder jumped onto the dock and secured the boat then came back on board and grabbed the heavy bags, leaving me with only my overnight bag and a light duffle to carry.

We disembarked and took the foot path up to the house. When it came fully into view, I gasped. "Wow. It's spectacular. Who lives here?"

"No one. It's a vacation home. But it's fully stocked with food and water. It's powered by solar, so electricity, heating, and cooling won't be an issue. There are fruit trees and a small vegetable garden. The bay is full of fish. You could survive the apocalypse out here."

Wilder looked and sounded tense as he let me into the home and showed me around. Surely he wasn't worried about a stalker finding me *here*? This place was about as off-the-grid as it got.

As we moved from room to room, I couldn't keep from oohing and aahing. Each one was more beautiful than the last. Huge windows let in the natural light and views of the ocean as well as the flowering shrubs and trees that surrounded the house.

Indoors, more flowering plants and potted trees anchored each room, filling the air with a fresh, natural scent and blurring the lines between indoors and out.

"You know, I never considered buying an island before," I said. "But maybe I should—or maybe I'll just rent this place whenever I need a private getaway."

"You really like it huh?" Wilder asked.

"Like it? I love it. It's perfect. Who owns it?"

"I'm not at liberty to say."

"Well, whoever they are, they have impeccable taste—or at least taste that was made exactly for me. I literally wouldn't change a single thing."

Wilder seemed inordinately pleased. "I'll pass it along. Want to see where you'll be sleeping?"

He led me down a hallway and opened a set of double doors to a gorgeous master suite decorated in cream and taupe and rich browns.

It was the first bedroom I'd seen. He'd shown me a workout room, an office, a powder room, in addition to the amazing kitchen and living room area.

A baby grand piano situated by the floor-to-ceiling window wall overlooking the ocean had caught my eye in that room. But I hadn't noticed any guest rooms or children's rooms, and this seemed to be the end of the grand tour.

"This isn't the only bedroom, is it?" I asked.

Wilder shrugged. "Only one person ever sleeps here, so it hasn't been necessary to have others."

"Wait a minute..."

I looked around at the classic, masculine bedroom, the huge, *man-sized* king bed. "Is this... *your* house?"

He shrugged.

"It is, isn't it? You own an island?"

Shrugging again, he looked down and shifted his weight. "Just a small one. The U.S. Dollar goes a long way here. I told you I was into privacy."

"So then this is your room— and that's your bed. I'm not taking your bed."

I picked up my bag and headed for the door. Wilder took it from me and planted it on the floor again.

"Yes you are. I insist. You're a guest, and it has an attached bathroom, so you'll have everything you need in the suite. It just makes sense."

"But then where will you sleep?"

"The office next door has a couch."

"That couch is way too short for you to stretch out on." I frowned. "I'll take the couch."

"Absolutely not. I'll be fine. It pulls out into a sleeper. Anyway, it's no big deal. Believe me, as a SEAL, you learn to sleep anywhere anytime, no matter how uncomfortable. Besides, we're not going to be here that long."

Right. Once again I was reminded that this was not a lovely tropical vacation but an obligation for Wilder—a chore. At best he saw me as Hap's little sister. At worst, I was just another client to him, and I couldn't let myself forget it.

Don't fall for him again. You're not a stupid little girl anymore.

My joy over exploring the beautiful house dimmed. "Well I hope not. How will you keep in touch with the mainland? You know, to find out when they catch the stalker and we can go home?"

Wilder pulled a phone-like device from his bag. "This is a global satphone. I'll check in daily with Gray at Veridian. He'll keep me informed."

"Could the stalker trace that thing and find me here?"

"Not unless he's top-level U.S. military—and has a hell of a travel agent. Don't worry. You're completely safe here. I want you to relax and try to enjoy yourself. Look at it as some well-deserved R and R after your tour."

NINE

Keyed Up

Wilder

I would *not* be resting or relaxing. I couldn't afford to let my guard down for a single second.

Not because of the stalker. What I'd said to Jessica was true—this was the safest place on earth for her.

No, I had to stay vigilant against a *different* kind of danger.

If I let my self-control slip at all, I was liable to do or say something I couldn't take back, and I'd lose Hap's friendship forever—not to mention what Jessica would think of me.

I was famous for my professionalism. So why was it so hard to maintain around her?

Several times during our trip here I'd forgotten my own mandate and found myself noticing and appreciating the way her long hair shined and floated on the sea breeze, the hint of color in her skin from being out in the sun, her delicious throaty voice, and the way her remarkable green eyes shifted from emerald to sage to malachite depending on whether the backdrop was the water, the sky, or the tropical foliage.

Fuck. Why did I even *know* that many synonyms for the color green?

Though I'd never admit it to a living soul, that was Jessica's fault as well. Inspired by her beautiful writing—and her even more beautiful eyes—I'd attempted some poetry myself back in high school.

Throughout the years I'd continued jotting down lines as they came to me in a small notebook I carried in my back pocket. No one had ever read them—no one ever would. They were just for me.

Though I didn't understand why, writing poetry helped me make sense of some of the more troubling aspects of my past and my current career.

It also helped me record and remember the joyful moments of beauty and inspiration.

I tried to focus on those moments when memories of the past haunted me.

Though she was unaware of it, our common interest in poetry had always made me feel connected to Jessica in some small way.

At the moment, I felt inspired to write a sonnet about the way her bare, pink-tipped toes curled around the lower rung of my balcony's railing as she stood on it, about her radiant smile as she gazed out at the view.

Stepping down from her perch, she turned to me. "I want to go swimming. Would that be okay?"

"Sure. Let's grab a bite first and then we'll go down to the beach."

We walked back inside and went to the kitchen. Jessica ran her fingers lovingly over the Viking Tuscany series stove.

"Ooooh, nice," she purred as she stroked its shiny surface.

And now I'm jealous of a home appliance. Well, there was a first time for everything.

"Oh, the meals I could cook in here," she said. "This house is a dream."

Not in a million years could I have pictured Jessica Bailey here in my private domain, but now it was a reality. And her appreciation of the house I'd built and personally furnished pleased me—probably more than it should have.

I'd never brought a woman here before, or anyone else actually. None of my friends or family even knew where my "private oasis" was, which was why it was the perfect place to hide Jessica.

"You like cooking?" I asked.

"I do. I don't get to do it as much as I'd like to—hotel living, you know? But I cook whenever I'm home in one of my places. My mom's an amazing cook."

"I remember. I used to love staying for dinner at your house."

"You were there for dinner a lot," she said.

"Well, when you're one of four boys, you've gotta get your sustenance where you can."

Of course the food hadn't been the main attraction at her house. Not that I'd admit that to her.

"My poor parents," I said. "Their grocery bill must have been astronomical."

"Speaking of that—are there any groceries here?"

I gestured toward the pantry. "Help yourself."

Jessica padded over to the door and opened it, making a sound of surprise. "There must be enough food in here for a year—maybe more."

"We won't be here nearly that long." *Please God.* "Anything look good?"

"Everything. I'm so hungry. You?"

She turned around and grinned at me, and the word *Yes*

screamed through my brain. Seeing her here in my house, rummaging through my kitchen, filled me with ravenous longing... but also with a sense of satisfaction I hadn't felt in years—maybe *ever*. Which confused me.

It also terrified me.

It took me a second to answer. "Starved."

We ate a quick meal then Jessica went to her room to change before the two of us walked down to the beach.

"Are those your trunks?" she asked, eying my shorts when we got there.

"Nah. I'm not going in. I've got to make a call to Gray."

"Okay, your loss."

She stripped her coverup over her head, dropped it to the sand, and ran toward the water in her bikini, splashing into the calm bay with the happy abandon of a little girl. However, the way she *looked* in said bikini was proof positive she was a full-grown woman.

Stop noticing. Don't think about it.

"Wow, the water feels amazing." Jessica shot a glance back over the curve of one tanned shoulder, causing me to yank my gaze back upward to meet her eyes. "Sure you won't come in?"

I cleared my throat, trying to force a response past the lump in it. "No, you... go ahead. I'll just keep an eye on you from the shore."

As if I could take my eyes *off* of her. That would have been impossible even if I wasn't acting as her bodyguard.

She dived under the water then came up again, standing in the shallow waves that lapped the beach. Slicking back her hair with both hands, she gave me a brilliant smile as the saltwater ran down her body.

"I've just decided I'm okay if we *do* stay for a year. This is paradise."

Or hell, depending on your perspective.

As for me, I fiercely hoped it wouldn't be that long. Jessica was too tempting to be believed, and I had a feeling resisting her would be the toughest battle of my life.

Turning away, I walked out onto the dock and pulled my sat phone from its case. Gray answered immediately.

"Wilder. Hey man. You guys make it there okay? Wherever *there* is."

"Yeah we're good. No problems. Now we're just going to hunker down. Unless you have some good news for me?"

Please tell me they caught the guy, and we can go home before I royally fuck things up.

"I'm afraid there's nothing to report," he said. "The state police said this guy was a paradox. He left the camera and rope behind, but no physical evidence."

"No DNA?"

"Nada. Which is weird. No fingerprints either. If he was that careful about covering up and leaving no trace, how could he accidentally have left those other things behind?"

"Unless it wasn't an accident."

"What do you mean—he wanted them to be found? What would be the purpose of that?" Gray asked.

"To scare her. Maybe he gets a thrill out of terrorizing her."

My jaw clenched, catching the inside of my cheek and drawing blood. I squinted at the warm, coppery taste of it, fighting for control.

"Maybe he wanted her to know how close he'd gotten so she'd live in fear of the next time," I said. "Of what he might do to her when he does get to her. He *wants* her thinking about him."

The idea of it got my blood boiling. Then I turned to see Jessica floating on her back, face up to the sun, and my blood boiled for another reason.

Was she *trying* to drive me crazy?

The sunlight gleamed off her bare skin, creating enticing

shadows in the curves and making her glow like she'd been dipped in gold dust.

She was so delicate, so soft. It would be so easy for someone to grab her and overpower her… toss her in a trunk, drive her out into the countryside or woods somewhere and—

My teeth ground together so hard my jaw was getting sore. I forced my mind back to work. "How's everything else?" I asked Gray. "How's the Hood project coming along?"

"Great. The old lady's a hoot. She's quite a collector, and her house is a masterpiece. You don't sound too good though. You okay? You sound kind of like you're in pain."

Jessica flipped over and swam across the surface of the bay, doing a slow crawl stroke away from me, her long smooth legs propelling her forward and her bottom bobbing just below the surface of the clear water.

I chuckled. "Yeah, I'm fine. I'm just a little… keyed up."

She dove under the water again. This time she didn't come up right away. I started jogging down the dock back toward the beach.

"Listen Gray, I've gotta go, but keep me informed. I want to know everything as soon as you do."

"Will do boss. Talk to you later," Gray said. "And try to relax a little. You sound like you're on the verge of a stroke."

Maybe I was. Jessica had resurfaced so I was no longer worried about her drowning. I was however a little concerned with the rhythm of my heart.

How was it supposed to withstand several days, much less weeks or even *months* here alone with her?

TEN

A Matter of Self-Preservation

Wilder

When we returned to the house, I checked the exterior then locked the door from the inside and set the alarm.

It was unnecessary—there was no question we were on the island alone, and my radar system would alert me if a boat was approaching the island when it was still miles away—but the lockdown routine soothed me nevertheless.

"Want me to make us some dinner?" Jessica asked, walking into the kitchen.

Her hair had air-dried into touchable waves, and the tops of her cheeks and nose were pink from the sun. Her coverup skimmed her thighs, drawing my gaze down her legs to her tiny bare feet.

Everything about her appealed to me more than any woman ever had in my life. The *last* thing I needed in this state of mind was to spend a quiet evening alone with her.

"Actually, I'm just going to turn in early," I said. "I'm more tired than hungry. You must be beat, too, after traveling all day and then swimming."

She nodded. "Not really. But if you're not gonna eat, I'll

just fix something simple for myself then take a bath and go to bed too."

And now I'm thinking of Jessica Bailey in a bathtub. Not good.

Picturing her beautiful body spread out across my bed was even worse.

"Goodnight, Wilder," she said sweetly, oblivious to the dirty turn my thoughts had taken.

"Good night. Sleep well. I'll see you in the morning."

The next morning, and for several days after that, I did my best to keep my distance. Even from afar, though, her powerful allure tempted me.

She started every day with a session of beach yoga. *Ask me how I know.*

If there was anything sexier than Jessica Bailey bending and stretching and twisting in the sand at sunrise, I'd liked to have seen it.

I mean, I'd *really* like to see it because I needed something to pry my eyeballs away from that sight.

Even holed up in my office "working" it was impossible not to hear her playing piano in the other room—or singing in the shower. The house was absolutely filled with her—there was nowhere I could escape her presence or her voice or her scent, an intoxicating combination of vanilla and ylang ylang that lingered lightly even when she wasn't in the room.

And the sunbathing. The fucking sunbathing was going to drive me insane.

Every day Jessica spent time lying on the beach or the deck in one of her vast array of micro-bikinis.

I couldn't take my eyes off her. Actually I had no choice—as her bodyguard, I was supposed to keep eyes *on* her.

But I liked it *way* too much.

Nights were even worse. By nature, I was a night owl, but since we'd come to the island, I was turning in earlier than my grandpa Henry. The AARP was going to track me down and start offering me early bird discounts before long.

It was a matter of self-preservation.

Seeing her curled up on the couch in a t-shirt and shorts, looking soft and warm and oh-so-right in my living room was almost worse than hell week during my SEAL training.

"Watch a movie with me?" she asked one night as she flopped onto the couch wearing a baby pink t-shirt that read: *Never too old to believe in fairy tales.*

She'd probably suggest a rom-com, or worse, some animated thing with animals singing showtunes. That, at least, wouldn't be hard to turn down.

"I found Bladerunner on Netflix," she crooned in a tempting sing-song.

Oh right. ***Of course*** *she likes sci-fi movies and Harrison Ford, too. Somebody please just shoot me.*

It was like the Universe had conjured the perfect woman and put her right in front of me—but just out of reach.

"Nah, I'm pretty beat," I lied. "I think I'll go on to bed."

Where I'll stay up for another hour or two staring at the ceiling and battling the urge to jerk off to the mental images you so generously provided all day long.

Jessica shook her head and gave me a wrinkle-nosed grin. "I never would have figured you for an early birdie, Wild-man. Your high school posse would be shocked to see how tame their fearless leader has become."

I'd been on my way out of the room, but I had to stop and face her again. "You know... I really wasn't all that wild."

"Are you not the same guy who jumped out of the third-story science lab window on a dare? And stole Eddie the Eagle from the roof of the school and put him in the principal's bathtub? I mean, you were a legend—not to mention a walking, breathing cautionary tale around my house. My parents loved you, but they threatened Hap within an inch of his life if he ever started behaving like you. And the girls..."

"What about the girls?"

"There were a *lot* of them."

Was it my imagination, or was there a hint of jealousy in her voice?

"Not so many," I countered. "I mean, yeah, I was flattered by the attention, and I was a teenage guy with opportunity. But I didn't take every one that was offered. And when I got to college, it wasn't too long before I figured out most of the girls were just interested in dating a football player. It had nothing to do with me—they didn't even *know* me. Believe me, that got old *fast*."

She rolled her eyes. "Tell me about it. Try being a recording artist. The few guys who can get past the intimidation factor and ask me out tend to be either narcissists or fanboys who don't want to talk about anything other than my songs and videos."

"You seem to do alright." I smirked.

Unless they'd been living under a rock, pretty much everyone was aware of Jessica's—*Jade's*—reputation with celebrity men. She'd dated actors, models, other musicians, athletes, and a famous Las Vegas magician. All of them had wound up in her songs when the relationships ended.

She shrugged. "So do you. I heard you were dating that actress, Bree Steele."

Now it was my turn to shrug. "Not really. We hung out a little after my protection detail for her ended. I see other people from time to time, but it's all pretty casual."

And *why* was I telling her all this? I wasn't sure, but I couldn't seem to stop myself from being honest. "My job makes it hard to have anything consistent."

"Exactly. Or anything *real*," she said.

"I'm sure. You probably love being home with your family and the people who knew you before you were famous."

Jessica's eyes went very serious, and she paused a moment before answering. "Yes," she said. "I do."

For a moment we held electric eye contact. Neither of us said anything, but there still seemed to be some sort of communication going on, something powerful and alive passing between us like an arc of glowing light and heat.

Finally I spoke, sounding short of breath, which I absolutely was. "Well, I'll... do my best to get you back home soon. See you at breakfast."

Jessica frowned down at the remote in her hand then at the TV screen. "See you in the morning, Wilder."

As it turned out, I saw her much sooner than that.

* * *

I was having a dream—a good one. I'd joined Jessica in the tranquil waters of the bay where we played a two-person game of sharks and minnows.

Naturally, I was the shark.

I was on the verge of taking a delicious bite when I was snapped awake by the sounds of a struggle followed by gunfire. I sprang off the couch and grabbed my gun, racing down the hall with my heart thundering in my chest.

Kicking open the bedroom door, I charged into the room, holding the weapon in front of me.

Jessica, who'd been sitting up cross-legged on top of the covers, screamed and flailed her arms in a startle reaction. The bowl she'd been holding flew into the air and flipped over, scattering popcorn all over the bedding.

"What is it? What's going on? Is someone here?"

My eyes scanned the room, moving from her frightened

expression to the large TV screen on the wall. I let out a long breath, and my pulse rate began to drop.

Shaking my head, I laughed softly. "You're... watching another movie."

She nodded, still tense and scared looking. "I was. Is everything okay?"

I set my gun down on a small table and walked over to her. "Yeah. Everything's fine. I was sleeping, and I heard battle noises. I was just disoriented there for a minute."

"Oh. Sorry it was so loud." She cringed an apologetic smile and looked around her. "Want some popcorn?"

Plucking a fluffy white kernel from the bedspread, I tossed it into my mouth, making her laugh.

"Thanks. So what are you watching?" Before she could answer, I recognized the movie. "Terminator 3? Really?"

Jessica held up a hand. "I don't even want to hear it. It's a great movie, and I like it."

I shook my head in amazement. "I wasn't going to criticize it. I agree with you. Although of course the original Terminator is the best."

"Of course," she said, as if it was ridiculous to think otherwise.

"I didn't know you liked the Terminator movies." Harrison Ford *and* Arnold. *Wow.*

"Love them. The concept is so brilliant, and they're always exciting and funny and romantic. I've seen them... oh gosh, too many times to count. What's your favorite? I mean, besides the original of course."

"I actually really liked Terminator Salvation, though I know a lot of people didn't."

"I *loved* that one." She shifted to sit on her knees, bouncing on the bed a little in her enthusiasm. "Sam Worthington and Christian Bale were so good in it."

She patted the mattress. "Want to join me? I can't sleep. We could watch that one next—this one's almost over."

For a moment, I was insanely tempted. I bit the inside of my cheek hard enough to make myself wince.

How stupid are you dude?

There was no way I could climb into bed with Jessica Bailey to watch movies—or do anything else—especially after that dream.

This was *not* a slumber party. It wasn't a date. It was a work detail.

And she wasn't an ordinary client. She was *Hap's little sister.*

I shook my head. "Nah, that's okay. I'm just gonna go... back to bed. Thanks though."

Her exuberant body language wilted. "Okay. Well... I'll turn the volume down so it doesn't wake you again."

As I turned to go, she called out to me. "Wilder?"

"Yeah?" I spun back around.

She gave me a sweet smile. "Have a good sleep."

Oh yeah, I'm just gonna drift right off to dreamland after this.

Jessica Bailey in my bed in a sleep shirt with her tousled hair was just about the sexiest thing I'd ever seen—on or off screen.

And I was trapped here with her for God knew how long.

Fuck. Me.

ELEVEN

Bodyguard Code

Jessica

Was it my imagination, or had Wilder just bitten the inside of his cheek?

I'd seen the body language "tell" many times when we were younger. He'd done it whenever my dad teased him about all the girls chasing him. When he'd received award after award at our school's senior honors night, I'd seen it again.

It meant he was uncomfortable—or stressed.

And he'd displayed the nervous tic just now when I'd invited him to join me in watching a movie in my room.

There'd been a look in his eye, too, when his gaze had run over my sleepwear and bare legs—sort of... appraising... or maybe appreciative?

My heart gave a hard thump. Had Wilder *finally* noticed me as a woman after all this time?

I snorted. All it had taken was thirteen years, a creepy stalker, being trapped together on a deserted island on the other side of the world, and Terminator 3.

Maybe he *wasn't* as indifferent to me as I'd always believed. I needed to know for sure. And in spite of the horror that had precipitated this impromptu hiatus from real life, our confinement here *did* provide the perfect opportunity to find out.

But how to go about it?

Wilder was so disciplined and controlled. And while I had a reputation as a "lover and leaver" of a string of good-looking actors and musicians, I wasn't *actually* a maneater.

I wasn't even all that *good* with men.

Those celebrity "relationships" had been set up by publicists. They'd consisted mostly of very public first dates and a few photo ops and had come and gone without much emotion on the part of the guys or myself.

The only one of them I'd truly liked—a super-cute member of a British boy band—had confessed he was in a secret long-term relationship with his high school sweetheart but had been ordered by his manager to keep it quiet to avoid spoiling his heartthrob status.

Having left high school early myself to work on the TV show, I hadn't even had a high school sweetheart or even many dates.

Since then... well, my life wasn't exactly conducive to relationships. My schedule was busy and chaotic, constantly requiring me to pack up and go from place to place for performances or publicity appearances.

There had been one short-lived relationship with one of my dancers on tour, but that had ended when I found out how many *other* "relationships" he'd had while on tour—before, after and *during* our brief affair.

Yuck. That certainly hadn't helped my self-esteem—or my confidence with men.

Wilder was different. Based on our conversation earlier tonight, he *wasn't* the player I'd assumed him to be. And as far as Hap knew, he wasn't seriously involved with anyone.

The question was... did he want to be?

And was there any possibility of that *someone* being me?

* * *

Over the next few days, I tried to feel him out. I invited him to swim in the bay with me and to stay up late and watch movies together—not in bed—on the couch.

Still, he turned me down. He *always* turned me down, always had some excuse, citing fatigue or busyness. In fact, he seemed determined to keep me at a distance.

I was pretty sure there had to be some sort of prohibition against security personnel and their clients having personal relationships—he'd mentioned he hadn't dated Bree Steele until after his protection detail of her ended.

But then Wilder and I weren't *just* a professional and his client—we'd known each other for years.

If he was interested, the "bodyguard code" or whatever shouldn't stand in his way.

Maybe I needed to just accept that he *wasn't* interested.

Feeling particularly mopey one morning and frankly growing bored of being isolated with only the world's most stoic guardian for company, I walked into Wilder's office and flopped down in one of the deep leather club chairs facing his desk.

He glanced up and gave me a perfunctory nod. "Good morning. What are your plans for today? Going for a swim?"

"No. I'm tired of swimming alone."

"Well, I wish I could join you, but I've got a lot of scheduling and expense-tracking to do for the business," he explained. "With Gray working on the Hood project, he can't stay in the office all the time. It's been piling up, but it's something I can do remotely from here."

Wilder cleared his throat, and his gaze darted away, retreating to his desktop, where he made of project of straightening the papers there.

The one in his hand shook a little. That's when I realized his fingers were trembling.

Interesting.

My belly did a gentle somersault.

"Sure. I understand." I gave an exaggerated sigh. "So, I know you don't want me to go down to the water by myself, and since you have so much work to do right now, I guess I'll just stay up here on the deck."

"Great." He smiled, looking distinctly relieved. "You going to work on some music?"

With an innocent smile, I said, "No. I think I'll just sunbathe for a while."

Wilder flinched. His jaw was so tight it barely moved as he answered. "Great. Have fun. I'll be... here in my office."

I'm counting on it.

When I turned around to go change in my room, I smiled. Because the sundeck was directly outside Wilder's office window.

And I still had one swimsuit he hadn't seen yet.

TWELVE

First Aid Not Foreplay

Wilder

What. The. *Fuck* was Jessica wearing?

As someone who danced for hours on stage night after night and exercised regularly, she was understandably unashamed of her strong, fit body. She'd worn some pretty tiny shorts and even tinier bathing suits since we'd been here.

That had been hard enough to handle.

But today's bikini took the prize. In fact, if I were her boyfriend, I'd feel like I'd *won* a prize.

My mouth literally watered as I watched her walk out onto the deck and spread her towel over one of the chaise lounges. From the front, the two-piece suit was sexy, turquoise straps holding the barely there cut-out top in place and suspending two matching pink hearts over the nipple area.

From the back... it was lethal.

The g-string design featured another innocent pink heart right at the apex of her firm ass. Which was now on full display as she lay on her stomach, facing away from me.

She was, in a word, perfect. At least as far as what appealed to me personally.

She had to know that suit would get my attention, right? I mean I was a professional, but I'd have to be blind and/or *dead* not to notice it.

Was that what Jessica wanted?

Without my permission, my dick responded to the idea. I shifted in my desk chair, willing the uninvited erection away.

She'd certainly warmed up and become more friendly since we'd arrived here, but she hadn't done or said anything overtly flirtatious. Still, she was used to a lot of male attention, and I was the only guy around at the moment.

God, how I wanted to give her some of my *attention*.

Then again maybe she was just trying to punish me for ripping her away from her exciting, glamorous life and basically marooning her here on an unpopulated island for who knew how long.

I wouldn't mind a little punishment from her either.

No. *No.* I had to get control of my thoughts.

Too late.

My dick was *not* interested in changing the channel. Instead, it turned up the volume and put the fucking thing on the vivid filter as images of Jessica's beautiful body filled my mind—even after I'd slammed my eyelids shut and banged my forehead against the desktop.

In my mental Jessica-on-the-deck-show, she reached around and untied the back of the string bikini then flipped over, propping herself up on the chaise and putting one foot on either side of it, spreading her legs so that miniscule scrap of fabric between them barely covered her lovely—

Fuuuuck. I had to leave this room and get away from that window. Now.

I strongly considered taking a second shower because a little me-time would have been useful at the moment.

No. I will not *jack off thinking about my best friend's little sister.*

Well, honestly, it wouldn't have been the first time, but I couldn't—could *not*—do it while we were living together and I was responsible for her safety.

Keeping my gaze trained away from the window, I unplugged my laptop and carried it to the kitchen island, settling there to try—unsuccessfully—to get my mind back on work. Truthfully there was nothing as pressing as I'd told Jessica there was, but there was a little paperwork I could do, some emails to answer.

If only I could think.

Which I couldn't.

So I gave up and went to my gym, running hard on the treadmill for an hour before riding the stationary bike and then rowing at top speed on my ergometer. I finished it off with some weightlifting.

Finally—thankfully—worn out, I left the gym, mopping my face and chest with my discarded t-shirt. I needed that second shower for a much-less-fun reason now.

The door from the deck opened, and Jessica stepped inside.

She stopped short, her eyes going wide. I looked down at myself and realized it was the first time she'd seen me shirtless—well, since high school anyway. In spite of the heat and humidity, I'd stayed fully dressed since our arrival here.

Now her gaze roamed over me, taking in my shoulders and arms then my chest then dropping lower to my abs.

I moved my t-shirt to my lower torso, letting it hang over the front of my shorts in case her eyes dropped any further. Because *fuckitall* I was right back in the state I'd been before working out.

Jessica was still staring—right at the place my t-shirt was hopefully camouflaging.

Say something, dipshit. Distract her.

"You... had enough sun?" I asked.

Jessica shook her head and let out a little giggle. "Yeah... uh... a little too much, I think. I forgot how much stronger it is in this hemisphere."

She glanced down at her arm as she took another step into the room, And then I saw it.

"Oh, shit, you are *red.* Did you not wear any sunscreen?"

She gave me a sheepish glance. "No. I thought I had a good enough base. Also... this suit provides a little less coverage than my others."

A little less... or a lot.

"So, I guess it exposes some parts of me that don't usually see the sun," she explained. "Now I'm not sure if I'm going to be able to even sit down."

She turned around to show me her back. Naturally my gaze dropped to her ass—which, while still pretty, was lobster red like the rest of her.

I couldn't suppress a laugh. "Oh man, you are... you are torched. I'm sorry. It's not funny. That can't feel good. I'll get you some ibuprofen for the pain and swelling. You should go take a cool shower to lower your skin temperature."

"I can't imagine standing under a spray of water right now," she said. "I think even a stiff breeze might hurt. I was sort of hoping to sink into a tub of strawberry Jello."

My body stiffened. *No. Don't go there. She's suffering.* Jessica needed my help right now, not my apparently uncontrollable lust.

I grimaced, fighting to suppress my overactive imagination and salivary glands. Strawberry was my favorite flavor.

"Afraid we're fresh out of Jello. I do have some aloe gel you can put on when you get out of the tub. If it looks bad enough, I also have hydrocortisone cream here."

Jessica nodded glumly and padded barefoot down the hall toward the bedroom. When she hadn't reemerged after an hour, I started to worry.

What if she'd passed out? In fact, she could have sun poisoning which sometimes led to dizziness, lightheadedness, fever and chills. She could be drowning in there. Why the hell didn't I check on her sooner?

Hurrying down the hall, I rapped on the bathroom door. "Everything okay in there?"

Jessica answered, "Yes. I just got out. I don't think I can put any clothes on, though. It *really* hurts."

The bathroom door opened. Jessica stood there wrapped in a towel. It was tan in color, making her look something like a freshly roasted hot dog in a bun. I schooled my expression and willed myself not to laugh.

"How're you feeling there, kiddo?"

She pouted up at me from a contrite face that was red but thankfully not as scalded as the rest of her. In fact, the front half of her body, while burned, wasn't nearly as bad as the back.

"Like I went surfing on a solar flare," she said. "I'm a big fat idiot."

Now I did laugh. "You're not big *or* fat."

She cracked a smile then winced in pain. "But I *am* an idiot. I'm going to be peeling for weeks."

She looked and sounded so pitiful. Any arousal I might have felt at the idea of her in the bathtub dissipated immediately, replaced by sympathy.

I handed her the bottle of aloe gel. "Maybe not. This will help. Rub it on your front side. Come out when you're done, and I'll do your back."

She nodded and shut the door again. While I waited, I opened the bottle of pain reliever and placed three tablets on the nightstand with a bottle of water.

When she emerged from the bathroom, I pointed out the ibuprofen and water. "Come lie on the bed." Then I added, "On your stomach."

"Ha ha," she said without humor.

But she obeyed, walking to the bed and crawling onto it, her breath hissing as her legs bent in the process.

"Ow ow ow. I can't believe how stupid I am. *Why* did I do this to myself?" she whined.

"I don't know." I chuckled. "Why did you?"

Pushing up to her elbows, she handed me the aloe and took the water bottle and pills I offered. She swallowed all three at once with a noisy gulp. Then she flopped back down, her head turned to one side as she lay on her stomach.

"Apparently I'm a sun-worshipper. *Was* a sun-worshipper," she corrected.

And apparently, I was a Jessica-worshipper. Because even now with her wet hair and her neon-red skin and that forlorn expression she wore, she was the most beautiful thing I'd ever seen.

The towel was wrapped around her torso, covering her to her thighs, so I went to the foot of the bed where I could apply the aloe from her ankles up.

"This might feel a little cold at first," I warned. "But it'll help."

"Okay."

Very gently, I began to spread the aloe gel on the tender skin of her calves. Jessica flinched each time I touched a new part of her leg, but eventually she relaxed.

"That feels good," she said in a slurry sounding voice. "It really is helping."

"Good. We used to use gallons of this when we ran missions in the desert and had to stay out all day doing surveillance. Okay, I'm going to do the backs of your thighs now. Do you..."

I had to swallow hard before I could finish the question. "Did you happen to leave your swimsuit bottom on when you got into the tub?"

Please say yes. Please *say yes.*

Not that the thing offered much coverage, but it would help me not to think of her as completely naked under this towel.

Jessica nodded against the sheets. "Mmmm hmmm. I was scared to pull it down over my legs. It's really bugging me now, though."

She squirmed and made a funny face. "Never wear a g-string—they are *not* comfortable."

I laughed out loud. "I'll keep that in mind."

Easing the bottom edge of the towel up, I carefully covered the backs of her thighs with the soothing gel.

"Okay, now the top half," I announced, hiding her upper thighs and the gorgeous curve of her lower buttocks with the towel again.

Jessica rolled slightly to one side then the other, allowing me to loosen the towel until it was possible to fold it down and expose her back to the waist.

Now the breath hissed between *my* teeth. "Poor girl. You're going to be sleeping on your belly for days."

She barely acknowledged my words, nodding gently with her eyes closed. "S'okay," she whispered.

I thought she might have been falling asleep, but when I touched her again to smooth the gel on her upper back, she took a deep breath and let out a long *mmmmmm* sound.

"Feeling better?" I asked, fighting not to emit a pleasure sound of my own.

Nah, that wouldn't be creepy, would it?

I wasn't a creeper. And I would never take advantage of the situation. I was touching her for medicinal reasons only—at her request. But it was still a little bit of heaven.

Her skin was smooth and incredibly soft. And very very hot.

Right. First aid, not foreplay.

I blinked and literally shook my head back and forth, trying to dislodge the inappropriate thoughts that had begun to sneak back in.

"Much better," she said. "That stuff is like magic."

"You're gonna need to keep applying it over the next several days unless you want to peel down to your skeleton."

When I got to the base of her back where that enticing pink heart peeked above the edge of the towel, I waved the white flag.

"Okay, I'm all done. You're gonna want to put some on your, uh... on your... flanks after you pull off that g-string, before you put on your panties."

Flanks? Really?

At that moment with my hand hovering, trembling, above her perfect ass, I hadn't been able to say the word. Even saying the word "panties" to her felt dirty.

Walking over to my dresser, I opened my t-shirt drawer and pulled out the softest one I could find. It would be enormous on her, but that was a good thing. She wouldn't want to wear anything tight for a few days.

When I dropped the shirt on the bed beside her, Jessica opened her eyes.

"Hey," I said softly. "I can see you're about ready to pass out. This should be pretty comfortable for you to sleep in. Feel free to keep it as long as you like."

She gave me a sleepy smile. "Thanks, but I'll just sleep naked. That's what I usually do."

I closed my eyes and let out a long exhale. *Fantastic.*

THIRTEEN

Selkie

Wilder

For the next several days, Jessica took it easy, staying mostly in her room.

Thank God. After that remark about sleeping naked I needed a few days of recovery time myself.

It was so much easier to resist Jessica when I didn't have to *see* her all the time.

But then I started realizing how quiet the house was. It had never bothered me before to spend time alone at home, but now the place seemed… lifeless. Empty.

Lonely.

Oh shit. I miss her.

That wasn't good. That wasn't good at all.

Lusting after her was one thing—missing her when I wasn't with her was another. I had no business forming any kind of emotional attachment to Jessica Bailey.

What was I going to do about this? She was eventually going to come out of that room and start parading around in barely-there swimsuits again. Hell, even if she was wearing a puffy snowsuit I'd find her attractive.

My problem was the real pull I felt to her—had always felt —was to who she was *inside.*

The next morning, Jessica came into the kitchen, barefoot and dressed in my t-shirt, which, as predicted, was enormous on her.

The extra fabric flapped around her, and it was the length of a short dress, so there was no reason—no reason *at all*—I should be turned on by the site of her in it.

Sometimes *should* just wasn't happening. I stepped behind the island to hide my hard-on.

"Sunburn looks better today," I said. "How do you feel?"

She slid onto a bar stool, propping her cheek in one of her hands and giving me a droll look.

"Like I've been to a lobster boil—as the star attraction. Actually, it feels much better today, thanks to you, but I still look ridiculous."

I bit back a smile. "No you don't. You look fine."

Actually you look hot as hell *wearing my shirt, but I'm not allowed to tell you that.*

"Liar," she said. "I look like one of those *don't be this person* memes. Thank God there's not another human around for hundreds of miles—I mean, other than you, of course, but you don't count. No offense."

"None taken."

"I mean, you don't count because you've already seen it." For a few minutes she was quiet, watching me cut up fresh fruit for her oatmeal bowl.

"I do appreciate your help. Sorry I've been sleeping so much and being such bad company."

"That's okay. Sleep was the best thing for you. As far as the company goes, I'm used to living alone, so I'm pretty good at entertaining myself."

Or used to be before you came along. Belatedly I added, "I'm glad you're feeling better though."

"I really am. In fact, I may even leave the house today." She laughed and wiggled her fingers in the air.

"Whoa now, don't get crazy on me. No, really, that's great. But I think you'd better lay off the sunbathing for a few days —for the sake of your skin." *And my sanity.*

"You don't have to tell me twice. I think I may become a vampire and go out only at night from now on."

"That's a good idea," I said. "Not the vampire part—but you could wait until sunset to go out today, take a beach walk, swim if you want to, at least until it gets dark. I'll go with you."

"Really?" Jessica's eyelids widened, making her resemble an eager little girl—except for the way she looked in my t-shirt. One look at that spectacular sight and there was no question she'd grown *all* the way up.

Encouraged by her enthusiasm and happy to see *her* happy again, I followed my oh-so-wise suggestion with a truly stupid one.

"I could build a bonfire, and we can cook out for dinner."

"I would love that." Jessica beamed. "I've always loved beach bonfires. They're so romantic."

Shit.

When the sun dropped low in the sky, I kept my word and accompanied her to the beach, watching from the shore as she swam.

As usual when it came to Jessica, I kept my clothes *on* and my dick at a safe distance.

After a few minutes, she called to me, treading water with her face just above the surface.

"It's so warm. You should come in. I mean, I know you don't really like swimming, but it feels great tonight. You could stay in the shallow water."

It took work to suppress a snort. As a Navy combat diver, swimming had been my life. During training, I'd swum for five and a half miles through Pacific Ocean waters that were literally shark-infested. I'd run missions where my team and I swam all night long. I'd dived to depths of 130 feet, dismantled underwater explosives, and held my breath for six minutes at a time.

Usually when I came to the island, I was half-dolphin, spending as much time in the water as out of it.

But swimming with Jessica would be more hazardous than any of my military missions.

"That's okay. I've got to build the fire."

As the sun set, Jessica's graceful form became a silhouette against the color-changing sky. She slipped in and out of the waves, diving under and resurfacing.

She loved the water so much—and I loved watching her in it.

Too much.

When darkness fell, she got out of the water, walking toward me, smiling and pushing her long, dark hair back from her face. Her wet skin shined in the flickering light of the fire I'd built in a pit nearby.

"You look like a selkie." The thought popped out of my mouth without any forewarning—and *without* my prior approval.

"What's that?" Jessica took the towel I handed her and started drying off.

"Nothing. Never mind." Why had I said that? I'd just compared her to a sexy siren with magical seductive powers. Out loud.

"Wait? I know. Aren't those sort of like mermaids? Mythical creatures who are like seals in the water, but when they emerge—naked from the sea—to lure fishermen to their death, they have legs?"

"Yeah." I coughed and cleared my throat. "Something like

that. You're a good swimmer. That's what I meant. When I said that."

Jessica just laughed. "Well I might as well be shedding a sealskin. *Look* at this horror show."

She turned to show me her shoulder and back, which were indeed peeling as she rubbed them with the terrycloth.

"At least you didn't have sun poisoning," I said. "We would have had to risk a trip to the mainland—and take a long, bumpy ride to a hospital."

I invited her to sit on the blanket in front of the fire while I roasted two sea bass filets in a steel grill basket.

For a few minutes, Jessica was quiet. She stared into the fire. "How much longer do you think we'll be here?"

"It's hard to say. I'm checking in with Gray every day, hoping to hear something." I glanced back over my shoulder at her. "Until then, we'll just have to sit tight and content ourselves with island life. It's not so bad, is it?"

"No. It's not. But I'm having a hard time not... I mean, I keep thinking about..."

Her eyes flickered to me and held for a second before returning to the flames.

"I'm running out of ways to stay busy," she finally said. "It's not like I can go shopping or even go for a drive. I can only spend so many hours a day working on my music and watching movies. You only have a few books here, and they're all about wars and military strategy. You took my phone battery so I can't even download any fun ebooks."

"I'm sorry. I know you're bored."

And I hadn't exactly been fun to hang out with. In fact, I'd been going out of my way *not* to be charming and entertaining. It was just like high school when I'd been deliberately stand-offish to her in an effort to hide my real feelings.

"At least you're safe," I offered.

"Yes, and I appreciate it," she said, but she looked miserable.

"What if we..." She paused, her cheeks growing pink. "Would you want to maybe go on a hike or something with me tomorrow?"

Damn. I'd successfully avoided swimming with her tonight, as much as I would have liked to. Spending a day hiking with her would be almost as bad. There'd be no office to retreat to when it got to be too much and I needed to hide my natural reaction to her nearness.

"I don't know... I have a lot of work to do."

Her shoulders sank, and I could almost see the energy leave her body as her spirit deflated. "Okay. I understand."

Her face wore that same crestfallen look she used to get when she begged to play driveway hoops with Hap and me and we sent her away.

The pull on my heartstrings was a physical thing, making my chest feel tight.

"You know... I could probably skip a day tomorrow. In fact, I could use a break," I said. "There's a pretty waterfall on the other side of the island. It's not too far, maybe a couple hours' hike from here. The terrain's a little rugged in a couple spots, but nothing you couldn't handle. You seem to be in... good shape."

Just like that, the life returned to Jessica's eyes and posture. Her smile was like a ray of sunshine breaking through the clouds.

"Running around a stage and dancing for three hours night after night will do that for you." she stood. "A hike sounds great. Don't worry—I can keep up. And if you want, we can start early so you'll be able to get back in time to work. That way we'll avoid the strongest midday sun."

"Listen to you, Miss Sun Smarts. I thought you were a night owl," I teased.

She grinned, rocking to the side so our shoulders bumped. "I'm a selkie, remember? And I think I can make an exception this once and get up before noon."

"How about before sunrise?"

Her eyes popped wide. "Really?"

"Yeah. The sunrises here are pretty spectacular, especially from the summit." I pointed through the darkness toward the island's highest point. "We've got to go that way anyway to get to the waterfall. Two natural wonders for the price of one."

"Sounds like a good deal," Jessica said. "It's a date."

I corrected her just so there were no misunderstandings—on either of our parts. "It's a *hike.* And be sure to bring a jacket—it'll be cold at that elevation until the sun comes up."

FOURTEEN
Wishful Thinking

Jessica

When I emerged from my room *way* too early the next morning, I found Wilder stuffing items into a backpack.

He looked up, his eyes performing that quick assessment they always did whenever he saw me. Zipping the pack, he plunked it to the floor next to the kitchen island.

"Good morning. Get a good night's sleep?"

"Not bad, considering I haven't gone to bed that early since third grade," I said. "If I'm ever awake at this time these days, it's because I'm *still* awake from the night before. I hope that sunrise is as great as you say it is."

He grinned widely. "It'll be worth it, I promise."

We ate a quick breakfast then headed away from the house and started up an inclining path that had been cut through the trees and underbrush.

"Did you make this path?" I asked, shining my flashlight around at the clearance in the lush tropical foliage.

"I did. Years ago."

"Too bad. I was kind of looking forward to whacking my

way through the jungle with a machete, you know, like they did in Romancing the Stone."

"I never saw that movie," Wilder said.

"That's because you're a guy. You should watch it, though. It's fun."

"Maybe I will. I guess that's one of the good things about being forced out of your ordinary life—time to do the things you've never done, to do things just for fun."

"That's true. This is the longest I've gone without working since I was sixteen. So what do you do for fun?"

"You're looking at it. I hike, I read about wars and strategy."

He tossed me a sardonic grin, and I laughed. I also swooned a little bit. When Wilder was relaxed like this, there wasn't a sexier man on earth. His smile, the sound of his voice... it all worked for me—big time.

As he'd warned, the hour-long uphill hike was challenging in some parts, but all the effort, sweat, and muscle strain was worth it when we reached the summit just in time to see the sun rise.

We'd walked through some pretty dense fog, but here at the island's highest point, we were above the cloud layer. Looking down on it from above was almost like standing on the shore and seeing the ocean. Blue and billowing, the clouds resembled waves crashing onto the sand.

The illusion was enhanced by the layered glow of purple, pink, orange, and yellow on the horizon. When the bright ball of light finally crested, I was almost surprised not to hear angels singing.

In fact, *I* wanted to sing, but I didn't. It was funny, I had no problem singing in front of a crowd of thousands, but the thought of singing in front of Wilder was intimidating.

When we were teenagers, I'd *wanted* him to hear me sing. I'd turned up the volume on my little amp while I practiced in my room, hoping my voice would lure him to me like a fairy-tale siren.

Instead, I exhaled a long breath. “It’s magnificent. Thank you for this, Wilder.”

Smiling, he looked over at me. And kept looking at me. After a minute, I started to feel uncomfortable. I let out a nervous giggle.

“What?”

He shook his head, and his gaze went back to the view of the valley and the ocean below. “Nothing. Just wishing I’d brought a camera is all. Ready to go?”

He got to his feet and offered me a hand up. The hike to the waterfall was easier. It was downhill, and there was daylight to help with navigating the path.

As the sun rose higher, I removed my jacket and tied it around my waist, comfortable now in my tank top and shorts. Birdsong filled the air, and the entire path smelled like flowers —we were surrounded by them. At one turn in the path, I stopped short because I could hardly believe my eyes.

A cluster of plants, about four feet high, were covered with tiny red and yellow blooms and...

“Butterflies,” I exclaimed.

There were hundreds of them. Some were black with what looked like a blue-green boomerang on each wing. Others were smaller and bright yellow with brownish tiger stripes. There were a few other varieties mixed in, some orange, some bright green and black, some with vibrant red wings that had blue and black spots.

“This is incredible,” I said to Wilder. “No wonder you like hiking. You’d never see anything like this in ‘civilization.’”

“It’s like a little Garden of Eden here. There are nineteen-hundred species of butterflies in Indonesia,” he informed me.

“Wow,” I breathed. “I’ve seen some on the plants near

your house, but this is amazing. What are these flowers? They're so pretty."

I leaned toward a cluster to smell them, but Wilder stopped me with a hand on my shoulder.

"Careful. That's tropical milkweed. The sap is a skin irritant."

"Oh." I backed up. "I've had quite enough skin irritation for one week, thank you very much."

Wilder laughed. "Here." He picked a much larger flower from a nearby bush and pushed it behind my ear. His hand lingered near my face for just a second, his finger brushing my cheek.

Almost immediately a butterfly left the milkweed plant and landed on my nose.

"He thinks you're a flower," Wilder said with a grin.

"Well, I know I don't smell like one—I've been sweating like crazy with this humidity."

"You never smell bad."

"Please." I rolled my eyes.

"No seriously. It's kind of weird. You literally smell good *all* the time. I think something's chemically wrong with you."

I pushed at his shoulder, and my butterfly friend took off, returning to his feast on the milkweed plant.

"Still… I'm looking forward to a shower when we get home," I said then quickly corrected myself. "I mean when we get back."

It's not your *home, Jessica. It's Wilder's. Even though it feels like you could stay there forever and be happy.*

The waterfall was gorgeous. Surrounded by pre-historic looking jungle worthy of a Jurassic Park movie, it was huge with a triple-step cascade that flowed into an inviting green pool.

Wilder slipped the pack off his shoulders and sat on a large rock near the base of the falls. Unzipping the pack, he withdrew two water bottles and offered me one.

"Thanks." I took it and drained it quickly.

"You hungry?" He pulled two sandwiches from the pack and bit into one, holding out the other to me.

"A little. I'll eat in a minute."

I pulled off one of my hiking boots then the other. Grabbing the bottom hem of my tank top, I drew it up over my head, leaving me in just my sports bra and shorts.

The outfit was completely modest compared to that ridiculous bikini I'd worn on Sunburngeddon day. But when I looked at Wilder again, he'd gone very still, his attention riveted to me.

"What are you doing?"

"Going in. We don't have to wait for a shower—there's one right here."

I waded into the pool, looking back provocatively. "Aren't you hot?"

His expression was serious—strained almost. He gave a terse shake of his head. "Nah. I'm fine here."

"Suit yourself."

Wading a few steps more, I reached water deep enough for swimming and dived under. I swam toward the waterfall, loving the feel of the fresh, cool water on my tired limbs.

"Watch out under the falls. The water pressure's pretty strong, and there might be sharp rocks jutting out or something," Wilder called.

I pretended I couldn't hear him over the rushing water. "What?" I waved to him. "You should come in. It feels fantastic."

Though he made no move toward the pool, Wilder abandoned his seat on the rock and stood, frowning in my direction. He cupped his hands around his mouth. "Be careful."

Smiling at him, I raised an arm high over my head, my thumb up in the universal sign for, "You got it."

Then I swam until I was directly beneath the falls. The cold water splashing down on me was invigorating.

In all of my travels, swimming under a tropical waterfall was something I'd never done. It wasn't on my bucket list, but it should have been.

It was an experience to be sure, but just like swimming in the beautiful bay, it wasn't all that much fun to do alone.

Feeling around and locating a large rock under the water, I climbed onto it and stood under the natural shower. I darted a glance in Wilder's direction.

His body was tensed, his fists clenched, and he leaned in my direction, poised and ready to jump in and save me if necessary.

Mr. Professional. Always on the job.

And then I had an idea.

Purposely wobbling a bit on the rock, I let out a little shriek and "fell" into the water beneath the falls. Then I stayed under, counting slowly... and waiting.

My patience was rewarded when I resurfaced to find Wilder in the lagoon, swimming hard and already almost to my position. Wow, he was a powerful swimmer.

He reached me and grabbed my arm, treading water and holding me up. "Are you okay?"

"I'm fine."

His face and voice were angry. "Why did you stay under so long? I thought you hit your head on a rock when you fell."

"I'm fine. I was just doing a little exploring beneath the surface."

"Exploring?" He huffed an irritated breath. "You scared the hell out of me."

I gave him a big smile. "What's the matter? Afraid you were going to get in trouble with your boss? Oh wait—*I'm* your boss. Or at least I'm the one paying for all this top-notch personal protection."

Wilder simply glared at me.

I kept smiling. "And as your boss, I decided that you should swim with me."

There was a long pause. "You were faking."

It wasn't a question but a statement, and a decidedly surly one.

"I only did what I had to do to get you to come in and cool off and *stop* being such a grumpy stick in the mud." I slapped the water in a playful splash that hit Wilder right in his beautiful, disgruntled face.

He swiped a hand over it to clear his eyes and slick his hair back off his forehead. "We're going back to shore. Now. It's going to rain soon, and I want to get home before the storm hits."

"You're making that up. I'm not ready to get out yet." I turned and swam away with a laugh.

A strong, warm arm slid around my waist, stopping my forward momentum.

"Stop this. I'm serious." The words were guttural and close to my ear as Wilder drew me back to him.

"So am I. You can't tell me what to do. I'm not a child, Wilder." With a hard kick and a wriggle, I was free and swimming away once again.

This time when Wilder grabbed me, his grip was like iron. "Then stop acting like one."

He dragged me back against his chest, one powerful arm clamped around my ribcage as he stroked the water with the other. In spite of my best efforts to kick and splash my way free, I found myself being towed to shore.

"Why are you going all caveman on me?" I demanded. "I was only having some fun."

"And I'm only doing my *job*—which is the *reason* I'm here."

When we reached the shallows, a crack of thunder sounded, and I looked up. Dark clouds were moving fast overhead.

Oh. So Wilder *hadn't* just been making an excuse to keep from swimming with me.

And what he'd said had been entirely true—he was only on the island with me to keep me safe. Today, the sunrise and the beautiful hike with the butterfly bush, it was all just part of his job.

Any discomfort or struggle I'd believed I'd detected in him was a figment of my imagination. Wishful thinking. The stupid dream of a stupid little girl who somehow still hadn't outgrown her stupid crush on her big brother's best friend.

The two of us trudged onto the rocky bank of the lagoon, dressed in silence, and started for the house. I had to hustle to keep up with Wilder's long-legged pace. But he looked back over his shoulder every few seconds, making sure I hadn't fallen behind.

Doing his duty.

Twenty minutes into the hike, the sky opened and pelted us with rainfall so hard it was difficult to see the path. Wilder stopped and put a hand on my arm. He leaned in so I could hear him over the din of raindrops hitting the thick jungle foliage around us.

"Hold onto the back of my shirt. I don't like not being able to see you, and I want to know you're still with me. I can't be turning around constantly. I need to look out for the safest footing for us."

"Okay," I sputtered against the water running down my face in sheets. "Wilder... I'm sorry. For pretending to be in trouble in the water—and for not listening when you said it was time to get out. I was acting like a brat."

For a second, he stared at me. "Let's just get home. Grab my shirt and don't let go."

He turned around and forged ahead without another word—without accepting my apology.

At first when I'd spotted Wilder swimming toward me, I'd thought I'd won a major victory. I had finally gotten his attention—and gotten him into the water.

In my imagination the scene had played out like one of those romantic movies or TV shows where a couple is stranded together and finds a beautiful lagoon where they splash and play and flirt. And kiss.

In reality, I'd only succeeded in irritating him, and now, in getting us both stuck outside in a potentially dangerous storm.

Ugh. I was such an idiot. I was embarrassed, too.

When were the police going to catch that stalker? Was it really necessary to keep hiding away like this?

I made up my mind to talk to Wilder when we got back to the house and were safe and dry again. The truth was, I *was* employing him, and it was my decision whether to stay here or go back.

At the moment I wanted nothing more than to be far, far away from Wilder Lowe.

FIFTEEN
Nurse Jessica

Jessica

Holding onto Wilder's shirt like a kindergartner in line for recess, I squinted against the pelting rain and trudged along behind him.

He occasionally gave some direction or other, but for the most part the walk home was quiet. It gave me far too much time to think about the error of my ways.

I was through trying to get his attention. I was through being pathetic.

I was through chasing Wilder Lowe.

After about an hour and a half, he said, "We're on the final descent now, maybe a half hour from the house. But stay right with me. We're coming up on the dangerous part of the path."

Suddenly, his feet stopped moving, and I pitched forward, tripping over one of them, losing my grip on his shirt, and falling to the ground. I was fine, but Wilder let out a grunt of pain.

"Are you all right? What happened?" I scooted over to him.

"I tripped on something. My boot's stuck." He grimaced,

holding his leg and looking around. "It's a root. I didn't even notice it."

He frowned at the gnarled root in the path and attempted to pull his boot free. "Ow. Dammit. It's wedged in there good, and my leg's at a bad angle. Help me get my pack off, would you?"

I stood and pried the backpack from Wilder's shoulders. Wow, it was heavy. He'd hiked all the way to the waterfall and back carrying this?

Setting it on the ground next to him, I asked, "What do you want me to do?"

"Find my utility knife—it's in the left pocket."

I found the knife and handed it to him. Wilder gripped the heavy multi-tool and pulled out a serrated blade that looked wickedly sharp.

Gritting his teeth and growling, he used it to saw through the root at the point where it emerged from the ground. Finally the pressure on his boot lessened, and he was able to extract his foot from the natural trap.

As soon as it was free, Wilder attempted to stand. He immediately collapsed to the ground again.

Lying back on the muddy path, he closed his eyes against the rain pounding his face. His chest rose and fell in rapid, harsh breaths. He looked nauseous.

I crawled close to him, peering down at his contorted expression of pain. "Are you okay? Are you about to faint? Are you going to throw up?"

Folding his arm over his eyes, he let out a long breath. "No. I'm not going to faint. I'm not going to vomit from a twisted knee. I just need to rest a minute before I try to put weight on it again."

"Rest?" I looked around at the jungle "Here?"

"I'm sorry. I know you're wet and miserable."

"No—I mean, yes," I sputtered. "I am, but it's fine. I mean, *please* don't apologize. This is all my fault."

Wilder shook his head. "It's my fault for taking a chance with the weather. I knew this storm was coming in today. I thought we could get there and back before it hit. Anyway, it doesn't matter. What we have to concern ourselves with now is what comes next."

"Right." I nodded rapidly. "So... what is that?"

"You're gonna have to help me get back to the house... unless you'd like to spend the night out here. I've got a pop-up tent in my bag. Always carry it just in case."

Somewhere over our heads, a loud screech pierced the continuous clatter of rainfall on leaves. It was followed by a clap of thunder.

"Um, no thank you. I'd much prefer to sleep in my nice, comfortable bed—I mean *your* nice, comfortable bed that you were so kind to let me sleep in."

"Well then I'm gonna need a hand up—and I may have to lean on you to walk. We're not that far from the house now, maybe half a mile."

"Sure. Of course. Just tell me what to do."

Wilder told me how to brace myself then, pressing his uninjured foot into the ground, he gripped the hand I offered and pulled himself to standing.

"Good job." He sounded a bit winded from the effort. Or maybe it was the pain. That made more sense.

It occurred to me I'd never seen him in any sort of weakened state before. Back in high school he was famous for never missing a game, for walking off any injuries with a stoic expression and an appreciative hand raised to the crowd when they cheered his return to the field.

He'd seemed god-like to the sports fans who followed his career—and to me.

But now... now he seemed completely human. Vulnerable.

It did something to me. There was literal pain around my heart.

"Now what should I do?" I asked.

"Come to my right side... good. Okay, I'm gonna lean on you and try to take a step. You let me know if it's too much, if I'm too heavy."

"Don't worry about me," I assured him. "I can handle you."

That got a chuckle out of him in spite of his obvious agony.

We started moving. Slowly. Not gonna lie—he *was* heavy. He was so much taller and larger than me. But I'd literally have died before complaining.

With each step, Wilder let out an involuntary groan of pain, and I felt it all the way to my gut. In fact, just hearing it had me on the verge of tears.

What a mess I'd made of things. Not only had I failed *spectacularly* to seduce Wilder at the beach—and the sundeck—and the waterfall—now I'd hurt him.

And now he would be even more standoffish than ever. He'd be even *more* inclined to view me as the annoying little girl he'd known way back when.

Real smooth, Jess.

Step by painstaking step, we made our way down the muddy hill to the house. By the time we reached it, Wilder was shaking all over and breathing like he'd just run wind sprints.

I opened the door and helped him inside.

"Help me over to the fireplace," he said in a voice that sounded like gravel in a garbage disposal. "I'll sleep there tonight on the rug."

"No. You should take the bed. You can't sleep on the floor with a hurt leg."

"No way I can do the stairs tonight." He chuckled then winced. "Believe me, I've slept in far worse places with far worse injuries. I'll be fine here. Besides, I need to warm up and dry off. You do, too. Maybe you can get a fire going for us? Do you know how to build one?"

"Wood and matches?"

"And kindling." He pointed to a small bucket containing short, blocky pieces of light-colored wood. "I'll walk you through the process."

I rolled my eyes. "I was just joking with you. I know how to build a fire in a fireplace. My dad showed me how as a kid, and I have at least one at each of my houses."

"Well, I wasn't sure. They might have been gas-burning. Or maybe you have servants who do that kind of stuff for you."

Wilder eased himself down onto the fluffy rug in front of the hearth, sighing in obvious relief.

"Servants?" I laughed out loud.

Selecting a few smaller logs from the wood bin on the hearth, I stacked them on the grate in a criss-cross pattern. "Do you really think Jessica Bailey from Eastport Bay, Rhode Island has servants?"

He shrugged. "It wouldn't be unheard of. You're a celebrity with a busy schedule."

"Well, I don't have servants. I do have assistants, but they're for the business. When I'm home I take care of myself. And tonight... I'll be taking care of *you*."

"I'm fine. I don't need anyone to take care of me," Wilder said, sounding embarrassed. But then a hard shudder worked its way through his body.

Reaching over his head to the couch behind him, I snagged the throw blanket and pulled it over his shoulders. Then I went back to the fireplace, arranged the kindling beneath the logs, and lit it.

"You should get those wet clothes off," I suggested. Then my tone shifted to something far less certain. "Do you need help... getting your... shorts off? And your... the rest of your clothes?"

Wilder shook his head, smirking. "No, I can manage."

"Okay well I'll... I'll go get you some dry clothes. What do you want? T-shirt and shorts? And underwear?"

"Just the t-shirt and shorts will be fine," he said. "I like to keep it simple."

I felt my face go hot. I was probably bright pink, too. Which was *so* stupid. It wasn't like I was some little tween just realizing boys had penises in their underpants. Some men didn't wear underwear, so what?

But it was different with Wilder—everything was. And picturing *him* going commando scrambled my brains into a fluffy hormonal omelet *right* at the time I should have been cutting cholesterol—and Wilder—from my diet completely.

"Um, sure. I'll be right back... with that."

I speed-walked from the room and went to the bedroom where I'd been sleeping. Not wanting to invade his privacy, I'd resisted opening his drawers. But now I had a legitimate excuse.

I quickly located the one that held t-shirts and the one that contained shorts and collected one of each to take to him.

In his top drawer I found a collection of mementos—some medals for military service, some coins from different countries, a couple of old baseball cards he must have saved from when we were kids.

And his wallet.

Looking around first, as if he was going to drag himself in there on his stomach and catch me, I opened it. Pretty normal stuff—ID, credit cards, a surprising amount of cash.

Hmmm. No condoms. Interesting.

From the top edge of one of the card slots peeked a dog-eared photo. I pulled it out to look at it and gasped.

This is mine.

It was a photo of Wilder and me and Hap from when we were young. I always carried it in my own wallet—for obvious reasons. I hadn't even realized it was missing.

How had Wilder gotten it? And *why* did he have it tucked in *his* wallet?

Hap must have given it to him. He must have wanted Wilder to have the reminder of why exactly he was here—why he'd taken the job. His lifelong best friend had asked him to.

Their bond wasn't the kind that was easily broken. It would take a lot to destroy a friendship like that—a fling with your best friend's little sister for instance.

Yep, it's time to go home. I'd nurse Wilder back to health, and then we'd leave.

When I returned to the living room, the fire was blazing. Wilder looked better. His face had more color and had relaxed, releasing some of the pain-tension it had held before.

Also, he was shirtless.

The large tattoo I'd noticed the other day on his shoulder after his workout was clearly visible now, illuminated by the blazing fire.

It was a skull with the tail of a rattlesnake in its mouth. Though the image was macabre, it was also beautiful. There was color—turquoise, even hints of pink in it.

Brushing the top of the skull was the tip of a feathered wing, which carried over to Wilder's back where it stretched across and met another wing. I wondered what it all meant.

"Hey," he said softly when he spotted me.

"Hey yourself."

"You changed, too," he observed. "Good. Don't want to put the golden pipes at risk of pneumonia."

"The famous Wilder Lowe sarcasm is alive and well. That has to be a good sign."

The shirt and shorts he'd been wearing were balled up on the hearth, and the blanket was now across his lap.

His naked lap.

Stop it. The man was hurt. Even if that lap was suddenly interested in me, I'd just made the decision I wasn't interested in *it*. And that decision was firm.

Firm. I bet he'd be *so* firm, so hard, so—

No. I wasn't here for that. I was Nurse Jessica now—efficient, impassive, kind but detached. And as soon as Wilder felt better, I'd tell him I wanted to leave the island and go back to my life.

I simply *couldn't* stay here with him any longer.

This whole experience would become a song, because—who was I kidding—*of course* I was going to write about it.

But that's all that would ever come of it.

Schooling my voice and expression, I moved toward him, offering the clean clothing. "I hope these are okay."

And why *do we sound breathless, Jessica? Get it together girlfriend.*

"Thanks. This is perfect." He gave me a sweet smile.

And what was that all about? Wilder didn't *do* sweet. My breathlessness was compounded by a few extra heartbeats and a headrush.

It was going to be one *hell* of a song.

"Do you want some ibuprofen or acetaminophen?" I managed to ask. "I'll bring you some water."

Wilder gave me an apologetic smile. "I was thinking of something a little stronger. I don't have any narcotics on the island, but I do have a bottle of rum. Would you mind getting it from the butler's pantry for me? And a glass. Get two if..."

His eyes changed, their usual light hazel color darkening. "...if you want one."

My heart fluttered. "Sure. Why not?"

Wilder dressed himself and made a quick call to Gray on the sat phone while I retrieved the liquor and his pain meds along with some snacks. I returned to the living room and sat on the rug beside him, pouring a finger of rum into each glass then adding some Coke to mine.

Raising my glass, I said, "To an *interesting* walk."

Wilder laughed. "To a strong woman."

"Strong... or chicken. I did *not* want to spend the night in the jungle with only a few millimeters of nylon between me and the night creatures."

Our glasses clinked together, and I took a sip from mine. Wilder threw the entire contents of his glass back in one gulp.

I encouraged him to drink some water and take the pain relievers then examined his knee. It was swollen, but not frighteningly so.

"My dancers would sometimes get knee injuries on tour," I told him. "This one doesn't look as bad as some I've seen. I think you'll live to fight another day, soldier."

Wilder laughed out loud. "Well now that I've been held up against *that* standard, I'm sure as hell not going to whine. My leg could be hanging off and I'd have to say I was fine."

"Hey—those guys are strong. You wouldn't even believe what they can do with their bodies."

One of Wilder's brows lifted.

"Not *that* way," I said, red-faced. "I meant dancing."

"Didn't you date one of your backup dancers?"

"Yes," I admitted. "And he was... limber. Unfortunately, he was also completely incapable of monogamy."

"Yes, I know. 'Casanova,' right?"

"You *know* that song?"

"I know all your songs," he said.

Sweet warmth spread through me as if I'd taken a gulp of hot chocolate—with extra marshmallows.

"So... is that what you're looking for?" he asked. "Monogamy?"

I thought about making another glib remark, but then I answered honestly. "Isn't everyone? I mean, yes, I've kissed a lot of frogs, and nothing's worked out yet, but I keep hoping. I mean, it would be nice to have someone to share life with—all of it, the real stuff—not just the stuff that happens in front of cameras."

He nodded. "I can see that for you."

"What about you? You said it was hard to have anything 'consistent' with the demands of your job."

Wilder looked down and quirked his lips to the side. Then his eyes came up to meet mine. "I haven't downed nearly enough shots to talk about my love life."

Lifting the bottle, I grinned. "Let me pour you another."

Suddenly, I had no interest in leaving the island.

SIXTEEN
Not Easy

Jessica

Wilder downed a few more shots of rum, while I finished my drink slowly. I knew my tolerance—not much—and I didn't want to miss a *thing*.

Unfortunately, he didn't suddenly open up and tell me all his secrets, but he did agree to watch a movie with me. Of course, he *was* kind of a captive audience, but still... at least he didn't seem to mind.

We sat side by side on the rug, sharing a cobbled-together dinner of fruit, nuts, crackers and cheese. As darkness fell, it was like we were the only two people left in the world, there in that little ring of warm firelight.

And I had a vision of what it would have been like to date him in high school—if he hadn't been two years older. And infinitely cooler. And my brother's best friend.

Both our lives had moved on since then—so far from where we'd started it almost felt like a different lifetime—but my feelings for him had never changed.

No, that was a lie—they were even stronger now. It was hard to guess what Wilder was feeling.

"Just one movie" turned into a Terminator movie marathon. We laughed and cheered, trading opinions on the series. And for perhaps the first time since we were kids, I saw him relaxed and comfortable.

Why was he usually so uptight around me?

I didn't *think* he was that way with everyone, and from what Hap said, Wilder was plenty comfortable around women in general.

So it was just me.

It didn't make sense. *Was* it possible the attraction was not one-sided? Could he also be harboring a secret crush?

That thought had my heartbeat rushing so loudly in my ears it was hard to hear the last few scenes of the movie.

When it ended, I looked over at him, drinking in the sight of his beautiful face in the flickering light of the end credits.

"I used to have such a crush on you when we were kids," I said softly.

Wilder's gaze whipped away from the screen to meet mine. "You did?"

His voice sounded strained, which gave me hope—and courage.

I nodded. "I think all the girls did, but I felt a sort of… ownership over you—I guess because you were at my house so much, and I felt like I actually *knew* you instead of just being infatuated with the *idea* of you like they were."

For long moments he was quiet, just holding my gaze as a parade of emotions passed behind his eyes. Finally, he spoke. "Jess, I—"

Next to Wilder, the satellite phone rang. He grabbed it immediately and answered. "Yeah. Hey Gray. Got some good news?"

Of course, I couldn't hear the voice on the other end, but I read Wilder's body language. It wasn't good news. His shoulders sank.

Strangely my spirits rose. I was no longer in such a hurry to get home. If the stalker had been captured, our reason for staying here would be gone.

"Oh. Okay, sure, yeah, I can talk to him. Put him on." Wilder's eyes darted over to meet mine then flickered away again. "Hey Hap. How are you man? How's Rachel?"

My previously racing heart slowed gradually to a normal pace as Wilder's conversation with my brother went on.

"No, we're fine. Everything's fine. I got clumsy on a hike and twisted my knee, and Jessica got a little sunburn a couple days ago, but other than that, it's been quiet around here. Want to talk to her?"

Wilder turned and offered me the phone. It didn't escape my notice that he avoided meeting my eyes directly.

Great. Just when we were getting somewhere.

I took the phone. "Hey there," I said in a cheery tone I didn't feel. "It's really late here—what time is it there?"

"Ten a.m. I didn't wake you did I?"

"Me? No. You know what a night owl I am. We were just finishing a movie."

I assured Hap I was fine, that I was safe and happy, if a little annoyed at having to stay in seclusion for so long. He told me he was staying on the Eastport Bay police about finding the stalker and reiterated his admonition to stay safely out of sight until they did.

"And listen to Wilder, okay? He knows what he's doing, and he's got nothing but the best intentions for you."

Well, damn. I'd been *hoping* he had something else for me—like the hots for instance.

But when I said good-bye to my brother and hung up the phone, I found he was right.

The cool, impersonal demeanor Wilder usually wore like a suit of armor had snapped back into place. There was no sign of the relaxed, approachable guy I'd spent the day with and had just confessed one of my deepest secrets to.

I wanted *that* guy back—desperately.

"What were you about to say?" I asked.

"What?"

"When Hap called, you were about to say something."

Wilder shook his head in a dismissive gesture. "I don't remember. Must not have been too important. Listen, I'm beat. I'm gonna try to get some sleep. You should too."

So he was just going to *ignore* my confession. Or maybe he'd already forgotten it because it meant nothing to him.

Dragging a pillow off the couch, he stuffed it behind his head then shifted his large body to the side, making an aggravated noise of pain and frustration when his knee moved in the process.

"Wilder."

He looked up at me, an apprehensive expression creasing his face. "Yeah?"

I hesitated as the words screamed in my head, *What did you think of what I told you?*

But I didn't say them aloud.

Instead, I said, "I really am sorry about today, about your knee. I feel so stupid. If I'd listened to you, this never would have happened. Here you are trying to keep me safe, and I've been acting like a fool."

His tone was gentle. "You're not a fool. I think you're just going a little stir-crazy being stuck here for so long."

"Aren't you? I mean, the island is beautiful, the house is lovely, but this isn't a vacation, and we're not some happy couple on a romantic getaway. You must be eager to get back to your life."

"Nah." He wrinkled his nose in that *no big deal* expression. "It's just part of the job."

The wording of his answer irked me. It was so blunt. So

honest. And it underlined what a fool I truly *was* to think he'd ever had or could ever have any interest in me.

"Well, I am," I growled, getting to my feet. "I'm sick of hiding."

Wilder bit the inside of his cheek. "Believe me, I get it. I don't want to stay here any longer than necessary either. I mean, it's not easy—"

He stopped right there, leaving off the end of that tantalizing sentence and shuttering his expression.

"What?"

He shook his head, his jaw tight. "Nothing."

"What were you about to say. What isn't easy?" I demanded.

His grim expression didn't soften. "Nothing. I've had too much rum."

Then he rolled onto his side, facing away from me. "I'm tired. I need to sleep now. You do, too. It's been a long day."

For a moment I lingered, studying the outline of his magnificent body in the firelight. Then I draped the throw blanket over him.

"Good night, Wilder."

He must have been asleep already because he didn't answer.

SEVENTEEN
That's What It Feels Like

Jessica

I don't know how he managed to sleep on the floor, but when I went into the living room the next morning, Wilder was still sacked out.

I made coffee and bacon and eggs, glancing over at him again and again. He'd thrown off the blanket during the night and removed his shirt, too.

In spite of his size and impressive muscles and the scruff of morning growth on his jaw, he looked sort of angelic.

Not in that feminine, fluffy way people tended to picture angels. No, he was definitely more of a warrior angel, fierce and terrifying but also achingly beautiful.

It was nice to be able to study him like this, when he wasn't aware of it. As I enjoyed the view, I kept wondering... what had he meant last night when he'd started to say, "It isn't easy...?"

The pathetic part of me that still longed for him wanted to believe that sentence ended with, "...being so close to you and not being able to touch you the way I'd like to."

The more sensible part of me knew it was probably more

along the lines of, "...being stuck out here for so long away from my friends and family."

Wilder was certainly not giving up any answers.

I spent the day indoors with him, making sure he was comfortable and fed, fixing his meals, keeping up with his pain reliever doses, and helping him to and from the bathroom.

In spite of the forced intimacy, it was like last night had never happened. He was back to his old detached and businesslike self.

But then several times throughout the day I caught him looking at me, and the expression on his face was... well, I didn't know what to call it, but it wasn't *un*interested.

Each time though, he'd looked away, the impassive mask snapping back into place.

He insisted on sleeping on the living room rug again that night. The next day, he was up and moving around the house in a sort of limp-hop that was slow and awkward but got him where he was going.

Which was mostly to his office where he stayed holed up working all day and for the next few days as well. Sometimes he went out to the dock to "fish."

I wasn't sure if his sudden "busyness" was a result of his conversation with Hap or my confession about having a crush on him years ago or both, but the result was the same—he was avoiding me.

Fine. I wasn't going to beg him to spend time with me. And I wasn't going to pout. I decided to take advantage of the opportunity to do those things I usually didn't have time for.

I dug up some milkweed plants and transplanted them closer to the house so I could enjoy watching butterflies from the deck. I read the war and strategy books, which actually weren't that bad.

And I indulged my love of cooking. The house was well-stocked with food, I had access to a spectacular kitchen and several cooking channels, and I experimented to my heart's delight.

One evening, I made several regionally inspired side dishes to go with the fresh fish Wilder had caught earlier in the day.

The menu included spicy jasmine rice, a green salad. I even attempted "rujak," an Indonesian fruit salad with peanut sauce comprised of star fruit, water apple, jackfruit, banana, pineapple, and bright red dragonfruit. The fish I simply brushed with coconut oil, sprinkled with pepper and sea salt, and put in the oven to bake.

As usual, Wilder was hiding in his office, but the scent of cooking food must have lured him. He appeared in the kitchen just as I pulled the fish from the oven, practically licking his lips.

"Smells amazing," he said, hobbling to the counter.

"I hope it will be. How's the knee? Looks like you're able to put more weight on it today."

He took a seat at the island, and I pushed a salad plate toward him.

"Yeah, it's getting there. Your fantastic cooking has cured me." He immediately dug in, tackling the fruit first.

"I'm glad you're enjoying it. I have to do something with my time, and it would be a shame to cook and then have to throw it all out."

Wilder looked mortally offended by the idea. "Don't throw anything away," he said between bites. "I'll eat it all. I can never get enough of home cooking."

I laughed out loud. "So I noticed."

After devouring both salads he polished off the fish and rice. When he came up for air, he said, "I heard you playing the piano today. I didn't recognize the tune. Working on a new song?"

"Yep. I think it's pretty good. It has a little bit of a tropical feel to it. Want to hear it?"

Wilder's posture stiffened, and his lips pressed into a tight line, but he said, "Sure."

Out of habit, I reached for his arm to help support him for the walk to the living room, but he shooed me away. "I'm fine. I can make it."

"Suit yourself, hero." I walked to the piano and sat on the bench in front of it.

Wilder made it there a little more slowly. He stood beside the baby grand, leaning on it for support and looking down at me.

Though I'd performed in front of literally millions of people in my career, I suddenly felt nervous. Maybe it was because he was standing so close, right there in my peripheral vision.

Maybe it was because this song, like so many of my other songs, was about him.

I began to play and sing. Wilder stayed silent, though at one point, I noticed his fingertips clench around the edge of the piano's lid. Was that good or bad? Was his knee hurting?

When I finished, I looked up at him.

The look on his face nearly stopped my heart. The stoic mask was gone.

His eyes, usually so cool and hard to read, were shiny with moisture. Across the bridge of his nose and atop his cheekbones, the skin was flushed.

After a few seconds he blinked and cleared his throat.

"That was... that was beautiful. Really, Jess, it was just... amazing. The melody and the... words."

I felt my own face and neck flush with pleasure. "You really think so?"

"Absolutely. Swear it on my life. I mean the writing is just... mine is nowhere near as good."

I blinked in surprise. "*Your* writing? You write lyrics?"

Now Wilder's blush covered his entire face. "Not really."

"Is *that* what you're always scribbling in that little note pad of yours?"

The top edge of the small leather-bound notebook he always kept in his back pocket was right at my eye level. Acting on impulse, I plucked it out and spun away from him on the bench, opening the booklet and hunching over it to keep him from getting it back.

"Let's see what we've got here," I said.

"Hey!" Wilder lunged toward me, grabbing for it. I slid from the piano bench and scrambled beneath the instrument, giggling.

"I'm fresh out of reading material, so this should be good."

Dropping to his good knee, Wilder ducked under the piano and swiped a large paw at me in an attempt to retrieve his stolen property.

"Give that back to me. I'm serious, Jessica. I don't want you to read it."

I giggled again, shifting the book to my other hand and holding it away from him. "Don't be shy. What's the point of writing if no one else ever sees it?"

Wilder was practically growling in irritation now. "The point is I do it for *me*—not other people. Now shut the book and give it to me."

He managed to get his fingers on it and tugged, causing the page in my hand to tear off. I gasped in surprise then laughed again as he tried to grab *it* from me.

"Don't worry," I said. "We can tape it—*after* I take a look."

I stuffed the loose page into my dress, tucking it inside my bra, then scooted out from under the piano and faced him with a teasing look.

"Come and get it."

Getting to his feet Wilder gave me a death glare and extended his palm. "Give it to me."

"I will..." I turned and started walking toward the nearby bathroom. "... in just a minute."

"No," he practically shouted.

But he was much slower than usual these days, and I easily beat him to the bathroom. I closed and locked the door.

He pounded on it, yelling, "Jessica. Open up. I'm not kidding around. This isn't funny."

Sitting on the closed toilet lid, I extracted the notebook page from my bra. I unfolded the warm, crumpled page and began to read.

And my mouth dropped open.

There in Wilder's small, neat handwriting were several verses of poetry. I turned it over to the back and saw several more.

Then I began actually reading them.

More shocking than the fact that Wilder Lowe had written poetry was *what* he'd written about. Or rather *whom.*

My eyes scanned the lines again and again, my pulse picking up speed and my breath coming in shallow puffs.

His words were about long, dark, curling hair and eyes the shade of jade stone, soft skin and even softer curves, about a voice as sweet as an angel's song and lips that he longed to kiss but never would.

My heart pounded in my throat. I felt lightheaded. I could barely hear Wilder's shouting and banging on the door now—my entire world had narrowed to the unexpected, unbelievable, absolutely beautiful words on the page in my hands.

What I've always wanted. What I'll never have.
Trapped with her.
More trapped without her.

And she will never know the eternal cage that holds my heart.

Is her sweet song.

The poem was entitled, "Hummingbird."

Feeling like I was moving in slow motion, I stood and went to the bathroom door, unlocking and opening it.

Wilder's hand was raised as if he'd been about to pound on it again. His face was red with fury.

But I wasn't afraid. Someone who'd written something like this about me could never hurt me. I held the page out to him.

"What is this?"

He was silent, but the anger drained from his features. It was replaced by a look of vulnerability I'd never seen him wear before.

"You were never supposed to see that."

"It's about me. It is, isn't it?"

He blinked and looked off to the side, then up at the ceiling, letting out a shaky breath. His voice came out sounding rough and broken.

"*Why* did you do that? I told you not to read it. I'm so mad at you, I could just..."

Before he could finish the thought, I slid a hand around the back of his neck and rose to my tiptoes, pressing my lips to his.

For a few seconds, it reminded me of our first kiss years ago, when I'd surprised him in my childhood bedroom. Wilder was stiff and unresponsive, as if he'd been flash frozen.

But then it was like some kind of internal dam broke. With a soft grunt, he wrapped his arms around me and pulled me to him, lifting me off my feet and caressing my mouth with a kiss so deep and charged with emotion it brought tears to my eyes.

His hands ran up and down my back, stroking my hair, shaping my waist through my thin knit sundress, then coming up to cup my face.

Every minute of it felt like inevitability, like it had always been meant to be. And it felt wonderful. I had literally never been happier in my life.

When he lowered me to my feet again and drew back to look at me, there was a whole new look in Wilder's eyes, something like wonder mixed with resignation.

"So *that's* what it feels like," he said softly.

My answering tone was gently chiding. "We kissed before you know. In my room, when I was sixteen. Or did you forget?"

He shook his head. "I didn't forget a thing. I remember everything when it comes to you."

The confession stole my breath. "Why did you say that then?"

"Because I've been wondering—pretty much non-stop—what it would feel like to kiss you again. Now. Now that you're not a little girl, and I'm not a stupid teenager who had no idea what he was doing."

I smiled and ran my fingers through the smooth, heavy locks of his hair. "You did a pretty good job back then, too. Or didn't you ever listen to the lyrics of 'Teaser?'"

"Your first hit song? That was about me?"

"Come on. You had to have known it was. I wasn't exactly subtle in my references."

"Well, when I first heard it, I thought maybe..." He had the grace to look embarrassed. "...but it's kind of obnoxious to assume a song is about you."

"You *were* kind of obnoxious back then. Or did you forget *that*?"

Wilder smiled. "I remember. So... what about now? You must not think I'm *too* obnoxious... since you kissed me."

I laughed. "You've grown up very nicely, I must say. And you *have* mellowed out considerably. You're not the Teaser anymore."

"Thank you for noticing."

"Mmm hmm. I noticed something else, too." I rose to my tiptoes again and nipped his lips. "I'm always the one who kisses *you*. You've never kissed me."

"That's about to change," he said before dipping his head and taking my mouth again.

EIGHTEEN

Shrinkage and Puberty

Wilder

I hadn't lied to her—I did remember our forbidden kiss long ago. How could I forget?

It happened on a Wednesday night. I'd been over at the Bailey house as usual, eating dinner with the family and then staying around to "study" with Hap—translation—we'd gone over our class notes and study guides for about fifteen minutes and played Xbox the remaining hour and forty-five minutes.

At some point during the game, I'd excused myself to use the bathroom. As usual, I'd bypassed the powder room door and snuck down the hall to Jessica's room, standing outside to listen to her practicing her guitar and singing.

Suddenly her bedroom door opened. I felt my face go hot and stammered something about stopping to pick up my dropped phone.

She smiled and asked me to come in, telling me she needed my help with something.

I'd always found it impossible to refuse her, so I stepped into her room, expecting her to ask me to help her hang a poster or get something down from her closet shelf.

As it turned out, she had something a little more hazardous in mind.

She told me she was rehearsing for a school theater production and needed my help blocking a scene. A *romantic* scene. She handed me a script, I read a few lines, she read a few.

Before I quite knew what was happening, she'd thrown her arms around my neck and kissed me.

And I hadn't stopped her.

On the contrary, if I was being honest, I kissed her back. And liked it.

The kiss went on for a while, changing from sweet to hot then growing slow and searching again as I used it to communicate my complicated, forbidden feelings for her.

As it ended, I stared down into Jessica's wide eyes and said the lamest thing. It embarrassed me to this day.

"Your eyes look like jade—you know that stone they make those little Japanese statues out of?"

And then I'd heard Hap's voice calling me from the hallway, and I'd jumped away from Jessica as if she'd been recently sprayed by a skunk. Hap had appeared in the doorway, looked from me to Jessica and back again.

"What's going on in here?" my friend had asked in a dangerous tone.

"Just some stupid play she's working on," I'd answered, striding quickly toward the door. "She wanted to tell me about it... like I *care*."

Both Hap and I had laughed loudly, and I'd left the room, not daring to look back.

As we walked down the hall, I added in a loud voice. "Hey, the cheerleaders are at Olivia's house today to paint banners for the pep rally. She said we should drop by. She is so fucking hot."

Hap had punched my arm. "Watch the language. My little sister can hear you."

I was well aware, which is why I'd mentioned the hot cheerleaders.

After that, I'd stayed far away from Jessica's room.

And then she was gone, off to Hollywood to star in *Just Jade* and after that launching her music career. I'd thought I'd never see her again.

I certainly never imagined I'd get the chance to kiss her again.

It was utterly amazing to feel her in my arms, to breathe in the sweet scent of her and hear the hungry little noises she made.

She hadn't done *that* at sixteen. Everything was different this time. We were two consenting adults, alone, with no chance of anyone barging in on us. Age didn't matter anymore.

She was a grown woman, capable of deciding what was right for her. And I was a grown man, experienced, and far better able to appreciate everything she was.

I *knew* what I needed and wanted in a woman.

And there was no doubt about it—*this* was the woman I wanted. Jessica was... everything. I had to have her.

Gripping the sides of her head, I pulled her close, my mouth hovering over hers before I plunged my tongue inside. It wasn't enough. I wanted to taste every part of her, touch every part of her. I'd waited so long for this—too long—and it made me frantic to have everything *now*.

Jessica seemed just as greedy for me. Her hands clenched my t-shirt then slid beneath it, coasting up my sides, around my waist to my back and up before coming to the sides again to push the shirt up and over my head.

When it was off, she sighed into my mouth, exploring my chest and abs with her fingertips.

"Oh my God you feel good," she breathed against my lips.

"*You* feel good—you feel *amazing*," I said.

Cradling her face and jaw with one hand, I explored her incredible body with the other. I gripped her waist, her hip, her bottom as I kissed her and kissed her, trying to communicate with my lips and tongue, and breath and touch just how much I wanted her.

"I've wanted this for so long," she said, expressing—as always—the way *I* was feeling inside with *her* words.

That was the thing that had tortured me about her songs all these years. It was like she'd already found my poems years ago and set them to music—not the exact words but the feelings behind them.

Then she'd broadcast my feelings for her to the world. I used to have to roll the car windows down when one of her songs came on the radio just to cool off.

"Me too, hummingbird. Me too." I moved my mouth to her neck, lavishing it with attention, intoxicated by the smell and taste of her skin.

"I've been writing about you all this time," she told me. "Not just 'Teaser.' A piece of you is in every song I write. You were always with me—everywhere I went, all these years."

I kissed down her neck to her collarbone, then pulled the strap of her sundress aside to expose her shoulder. It was an insubstantial little dress, but even that felt like too much of a barrier between us.

Jessica must have been thinking the same thing because she pulled away for a second, reached down and grabbed the hem of the dress, then drew it up and over her head.

She stood before me now in just a bra and panties. I had to smile, running my hands through my hair and shaking my head. Was this even real?

"And you were always torturing me—no matter where I was," I said. "It was like no matter where I went in the world, you were there, reaching out to me with your voice, making sure I could never forget you."

She smiled back, a tentative expression.

"I'm glad you didn't forget me," she whispered. "Because I always wanted you, Wilder. I still do."

That was it. I couldn't take any more. I lunged for her, pinning her against the wall and kissing her like I was going to devour her. In fact, that's what I wanted to do—consume her, pull her inside of me so nothing could ever get to her, no one could ever hurt her or take her away from me.

Jessica kissed me with equal intensity, grinding herself against my thigh and pressing her breasts against my ribcage in an invitation I was powerless to resist.

"Wait," she breathed. She quickly unhooked and removed her bra.

I smiled, relishing the full access to her beautiful breasts. Palming one, I stroked the erect nipple with my thumb while my other hand delved into those little panties.

"Oh God you're wet," I said against her mouth.

"For you," she panted. "I've been running around this island every day for the past month with wet panties... because of you."

Oh fuck.

Sliding my fingers through all that delicious wetness, I pressed two of them against the front of her where she was swollen and throbbing. Then I started a slow, circular rhythm I didn't intend to stop until she was screaming and writhing on my hand.

Jessica's knees went weak. I slid an arm behind her back to support her and dipped my head to her breast, never ceasing the steady circular rub.

When my tongue touched her nipple, Jessica gasped and the breathy sound became an erotic chant of *yesses* and *ohmygods* and a repetition of my name.

wilder wilder wilder

Hearing her say it like that—hearing that angelic voice

ragged with pleasure and desire for me was almost too much. My dick was so hard it was nearly painful.

But I ordered it to stand down because nothing was going to stop me from making this woman come.

That—*that* was a sound I absolutely had to hear from Jessica.

She rocked into my hand harder, faster, and I picked up the pace of my stroking as I licked and sucked the sensitive tip of one breast then moved to the other.

Her breaths came faster, hitched, and then her whole body went rigid.

Panting and making the most erotic moans and whimpers I'd ever heard in my life, Jessica went wild. Her hands gripped my arm and shoulder, her nails pressing hard into my skin, and she cried out my name.

It was a moment I'd never forget as long as I lived.

When she opened her eyes, she gave me a sexy smile. "That was incredible. I didn't even know fingers could *do* that."

I grinned back, amused at her pleasure-drunk state. "That was only two of them. Just imagine what I can do with all ten."

Her smile widened, then her gaze dropped, running down my chest and abs to my pants. She reached out a hand, gliding her fingers up and down the erection straining against them.

"I'm more interested in what you can do with *this*."

Unbuttoning and unzipping my shorts, she slid her hand inside. My breath left me in a rush as she gripped my shaft.

I had to brace myself with both palms on the wall because *fuck* that felt good.

My body was on absolute adrenaline and testosterone overload.

Jessica Bailey has her fingers wrapped around my cock.

It was unreal, but it was also happening. My mind was fucking blown. I had *never* been this turned on before.

She worked her hand up and down the length of me, nuzzling her face against my neck. "You feel amazing. I had no idea you were this big."

That got a chuckle out of me, in spite of my aroused state. "Did you think I was hung like a baby kosher snacking pickle or something?"

Jessica laughed out loud. "No. No, but I saw you one time when you came in from the pool at our house and you were changing out of your swim trunks in the laundry room."

"How long ago was that?"

She looked up and rolled her lips inward, thinking. "Let's see... yours was the first penis I ever saw other than my brother's. I was about... I think I was eleven, so you would have been thirteen I guess."

Now I laughed. "You've been judging me all this time based on what I looked like at thirteen years old? Straight out of the pool? Have you never heard of shrinkage, woman? Or puberty?"

We both cracked up and laughed until tears streamed down our faces.

Jessica, who still had her fingers wrapped around me, stroked upward, making me groan and shudder.

"Puberty was *good* to you."

All laughter ceased. Delving my fingers into her hair, I pulled her mouth to mine and kissed her again. It was a lewd, wet, carnal kiss full of intention.

I was going to show Jessica *exactly* how much had changed since we'd been kids together.

Then after she'd had a few minutes to rest, I would demonstrate again. And again.

And again.

I pushed my shorts off my hips and let them fall to the floor, stepping forward and pressing her back to the wall again as I hooked my fingers under the straps of her panties and yanked them down.

Moaning in excitement, she tugged me harder. “I want you inside me. Let’s go to the bedroom.”

Hell yes.

Kissing her like she was the only source of oxygen left on earth, I put my hands on her hips and started guiding her backward toward her room. My room. Whatever—it was going to be *our* room from this point forward.

We’d made it to the threshold when somewhere in the back of my brain, the awareness of reality stirred.

Then it kicked, struggling to get back to the surface from the extreme depths to which I’d banished it in the past few minutes.

Oh shit.

Tapping inner strength I hadn’t been aware I possessed, I pulled away from Jessica and broke our kiss.

“We should... I need to stop.”

She blinked as if waking from a hypnotic state. “Why? Are you okay? Is it your knee?”

"No.” I smiled. “It’s fine. In fact, I sort of forgot I *have* knees. All the nerves in my body are pretty focused on another part of my anatomy.”

Jessica smiled, looking very pleased with herself and reaching for my cock again. “I don’t blame them. I may never be able to focus on anything else.”

Fingers shaking with the effort of restraint, I gripped her hand and stopped her. “Hold on a minute. As much as I’d love to, we can’t. I didn’t even think about it until just now, but... I don’t have any condoms.”

“None?”

“Not a single one on this whole fucking island.”

“Oh.” She paused a moment then repeated herself. “Oh.”

“Right.” I dropped my chin to my chest, cursing myself.

"I guess that makes sense—you said you're always alone when you come here, and this time, bringing *me* here, you had no idea this would happen."

"Exactly. I was determined it *wasn't* going to happen. In fact, I still can't even believe it's happening. It probably shouldn't be."

"Don't say that." She took my hand and stretched up to pepper my face with kisses. "I'm so happy it is. I've been wanting this for years. And no one's ever made me feel like you did just now."

"Really?" I slid an arm around her back, pulling her closer.

She nodded. "Really. All I want to do is do it again. And make you feel good too." She placed a hand on my chest, dragging it down to my abdomen.

Taking her face in my hands, I kissed her, slowly, deeply, my tongue demonstrating what I desperately wished I could do to her with my body.

When the kiss ended, I smiled down into Jessica's upturned face.

"Come with me. I have an idea."

NINETEEN
Horny Pirates

Jessica

"Where are we going?"

Pulling me by the hand, Wilder led me out of the house. "You'll see."

"But we're naked."

He grabbed a couple of the beach towels from a stack on the bench by the door. "We won't need clothes for this."

The night air was so warm, we actually *didn't* need them, but still it felt strange to walk down the path to the beach with no clothes on at all.

It also felt kind of amazing.

The breeze on my bare skin was comforting and stirring at the same time. I had a sense of freedom like I'd rarely felt in my life.

And the feel of Wilder's big hand wrapped around mine was almost too good to be real. It was like I was having a dream while fully awake.

When I glanced over at him, the sight of his big, muscular body gilded by moonlight really was the stuff of dreams.

I'm naked on the beach with Wilder Lowe. A little giggle escaped my mouth.

"What's so funny?" He grinned.

"Nothing. I'm just happy."

We reached the water and stood with our toes in the surf.

"I've never been swimming in the ocean naked. Or at night," I told him.

"I've swum in oceans at night before." Wilder chuckled. "Never naked though. Usually I had on a wetsuit and about sixty pounds of gear."

I squeezed his hand. "You never talk about your time as a SEAL."

Wilder looked out over the dark, rolling water. "There were a lot of good times. A lot of good guys and strong bonds —you know a bunch of the guys from my team work for me now at Viridian, right? But it all ended so badly. It's amazing how the actions of one bad apple can spoil it all for the good ones. I don't really like to talk about it."

I nodded in understanding. Though I was wildly curious about the incident that had ended his military career, I wouldn't press. He'd tell me when he was ready. But I did have to know about one thing.

"Is that why you don't like to swim?"

Now Wilder laughed out loud. "I love to swim. I just didn't want to swim with *you*."

My head jerked back in surprise. "Why not?" Grasping for possible explanations, I said, "Shrinkage?"

Wilder's laugh turned into a roar. He literally bent over laughing, unable to speak for a minute. When he was upright again, he swiped at his eyes, letting out a few more bubbles of laughter and a long breath.

He tugged at my hand, urging me to walk into the water with him.

"Shrinkage wasn't my concern. Actually I was worried about the *opposite* scenario."

At my quizzical look he went on. "Not sure if you've noticed, but since we've been here, I've been sporting more hard-ons than a fifteen-year-old at a stripper convention. Just looking at you is enough to do it for me, but it's also your voice, the way you smell..."

We reached water deep enough to swim in, and my feet lifted off the sand. Wilder kept me afloat, tugging me deeper. I think I could have floated without his help—or without treading water.

The things he was saying about me... and the knowledge that I turned him on made me feel like I could rise up out of the ocean and fly across the starlit sky.

Tensing my bicep, I pulled myself against his hard, wet body until our limbs tangled and our chests rose and fell in sync.

"So... you thought if your swim trunks got wet, I'd see."

He nodded. "Or feel it. I mean, if we were swimming close like this or horsing around in the water or something. I was afraid you might drift into me accidentally or touch me innocently, and suddenly the one-eyed creature from the blue lagoon would appear."

I laughed. "I think you're mixing up your movies there."

Wilder laughed, too. "Whatever. You know what I'm saying. I didn't want to offend you. Or start anything."

Caressing his heavily muscled neck and shoulder, I pressed my lips to his cheekbone, tasting salt.

"I *definitely* wouldn't have been offended. Surprised, maybe. You've got a good poker face. I had no idea you were interested."

"Interested? Try obsessed. I watched more episodes of *Just Jade* than any straight man should ever admit to."

I giggled. "Your secret is safe with me. Seriously, though. I was trying everything I could think of to *make* you notice me. If you wanted me, you did an amazing job hiding it."

"There's no *if* about it." Wilder pulled me tightly against him, letting me feel the evidence of his desire. "I *did* want you. I do."

He kissed me, and I drifted with him, not caring where the tide took us. Clinging to his long, powerful body, I knew I couldn't be safer physically.

Emotionally, I was in deep. My heart would never be the same after this night.

There was no one in the world like Wilder Lowe—there never had been and never would be.

"Do you trust me?" he asked between kisses.

I nodded. "I do. With my life."

After another brief kiss, he said, "Good. I want to try something. Ever floated on your back?"

"Oh, I don't float," I assured him. "I sink. Like a big old rock."

He laughed. "Everyone can float—little kids, grandmas—even sexy singers who think they can't. You don't have a ton of body fat, so it won't be as easy for you as it is for some people, but you can do it."

"Why? I don't want a swim lesson right now," I whined. Then I plastered myself to him and kissed him again, trying to distract him from whatever it was he had in mind.

Wilder wasn't dissuaded. Gently, he pushed me away from him until I was treading water on my own.

"Try it for me, okay? There'll be a reward in it for you."

For a moment I just stared at him. I did *not* want to do this. But I also didn't want to disappoint him. It seemed to be important to him for some reason.

"Fine. But if I wind up with a belly full of saltwater, you're the one who's going to have to hold my hair back all night long."

"Duly noted," he said with a grin. "Okay lean your head back and use the water as a pillow. Get a deep breath. Now arch your back to bring your lungs to the surface."

I followed his instructions and did actually manage to get at least the top half of my body to stay near the top of the water.

"Like this?"

Wilder stood near me, not touching me but watching closely. "Yes. You're doing great. Now drive your hips and belly button up toward the sky. Raise your arms over your head."

I did as he said but suddenly became self-conscious about my lack of swimwear. That raised chest and pelvis? They were fully exposed to the moonlight, and it was a bright night. I darted my eyes over at Wilder.

"Don't look at me, hummingbird—keep your head back and your eyes up on the stars," he commanded. "Now stretch your arms to the sides, palms facing up to the sky. And spread your legs like a starfish. Good."

He moved from my side to a point in front of me, positioning himself between my widespread legs.

"What are you doing?" I asked, starting to lift my head.

"Don't lift your head, sweetheart. You'll sink. Just trust me. Relax—tensing your muscles makes you go heavy. Just keep looking up and imagine yourself being light as a feather."

I obeyed and focused on the night sky, on the sound of the water gently lapping my ears and cheeks.

"Okay, you got it? You good?" Wilder asked.

"Yes, I'm good," I answered. And it was true. I felt entirely relaxed, weightless, and safe.

It was a novel thing to realize there was nowhere else in the world I would rather be—and no one else I'd rather be with.

There was nothing I wanted, nothing I needed... except for

condoms. I wished I'd somehow thought to buy some and bring them. I wished—

Goosebumps erupted all over my skin when I felt the front of Wilder's body along the back of mine.

He had dived under the water and was stretched out directly beneath me. And then he touched me.

His hands skimmed down the sides of my body from my armpits to my outer thighs then swept up again over the front of me, caressing the tops of my thighs, my belly and breasts.

He kissed the back of my neck where my hair floated away from it and did the mesmerizing move again.

It was like being ravished by a merman. I was simultaneously cooled by the water and night air and broiling from the inside out.

The tips of my breasts contracted tightly, desperate to be touched by him again, and between my legs there was a warmth that would easily have attracted any heat-seeking missiles that happened to be passing over the region.

A swirling current moved beneath me, and Wilder resurfaced. Lifting my head, I saw his face half-submerged, directly between my thighs. He planted a long open-mouthed kiss there, the heat of his tongue a searing contrast to the cool ocean water.

Tensing all over and unable to tear my eyes away, I started to sink.

Wilder's hand pushed my bottom up again, and his mouth broke contact with my intimate skin. "Remember what I told you. Keep your eyes on the stars."

I was going to see *all kinds* of stars in a minute if he kept doing what he was doing.

"How can you breathe?" I asked. "You're going to drown."

His laughter floated across the top of the gentle waves.

"Death by cunnilingus. There are worse ways to go. I'm a frogman, Jess. Didn't you know we could breathe underwater?"

"Seriously?" At this point I would have believed he was capable of anything.

"No, not really. But I did train to hold my breath for a *very* long time." He went back to work, and I threw my head back, drowning in sensation while attempting not to drown literally.

As my inner muscles began to tighten and my heart rate ratcheted higher, I said, "How long?"

Wilder stopped for a second. "What?"

"How long can you hold your breath?" I started sinking again.

Lifting my thighs and propping them over each of his shoulders, he reached up and rubbed my stomach with a soothing touch.

"Long enough. Listen, I'll worry about breathing. You just worry about staying afloat." He let out a snicker before adding, "And not screaming so loud you summon the Coast Guard."

Oh my god. This man was going to kill me.

Wilder kissed me again where I most wanted him, licking and sucking in a counter rhythm to the water splashing between my legs. I'd never felt anything like it.

If other people started figuring this out, beaches were about to get a *whole lot* more popular than they already were.

The pleasure built, creating waves inside and out, until I was a human tsunami, sensation cresting and splashing down, leaving me washed up on the beach like some exhausted castaway after a shipwreck.

And no, the Coast Guard didn't respond—but only because this wasn't America, and the Coast Guard wasn't a thing here.

* * *

We lay on the beach towels, me with my leg thrown bonelessly over Wilder's and my cheek resting on his chest, him with one arm wrapped around my back and the other hand stroking my wet hair and skin.

"If this security company gig doesn't work out, you could make a killing giving 'floating lessons' to women," I informed him.

He laughed, his warm chest rising and falling under my ear. "I don't hand out my top-secret training methods to just anyone. Only very special clientele—the ones I've been lusting after half my life."

His fingers drifted over my shoulder and arm, raising baby hairs that glistened in the moonlight. "You are so fucking gorgeous, Jess. And you're even better in bed than I dreamed you'd be—which is saying a lot."

I huffed a laugh. "We haven't even been near a bed yet."

"Yet," he repeated in a slightly threatening tone.

Staring at the stars above and the tops of the palm trees swaying in the breeze I gave voice to the thought that had been circulating through my brain since our first kiss—well, our first kiss on the island.

Our first kiss as teenagers had apparently ruined me for life, branding me for Wilder's sole possession and making it impossible for me to find a real, lasting connection with anyone else.

"I don't ever want to leave here," I said. "All I want to do is stay here with you and swim and make love and drink rum like a couple of horny pirates. There *were* female pirates, you know."

Wilder was quiet. Finally, he said, "I think we should talk."

Well *that* didn't sound good. I nodded, tracing an infinity pattern on his chest with my fingernail. "Okay. What are you thinking?"

"Honestly?" He gave a self-deprecating laugh, scrubbing a

hand through the hair on the top of his head before lying back on his palm again. "I'm thinking I want to go down on you again. Every. Fucking. Day. You are so unbelievably beautiful and sexy and—well, I'd better stop there, I think. What we *should* talk about is what we're going to do about *this*."

I lifted my head to look at his face. "And what exactly *is* this?"

"Well, on my part... it's been a long time coming," he said. "I've always liked you, Jess. I've always been attracted to you, like, a ridiculous amount. But obviously, I couldn't do anything about it."

"Because?"

"Well, your brother's my best friend. And you were too young for me... back then. I should never have kissed you that first time, but you surprised me, and you were so fucking cute and sexy."

"And now? Should you have kissed me now?" I asked, pleased by his assessment of teenaged me.

"Definitely not. But I did it anyway. Well, to be fair, you kissed me first... but I wanted you to."

I smiled against his delicious warm skin. "And then *you* kissed *me*. Finally."

"Yes. I did. But I'm not sure where we go from here. I've been devoting so much energy to resisting you, I'm not sure what to do now."

"*Stop* resisting me?" I suggested.

He laughed. "Yeah, well you see that's where things get a little sticky. It might be all well and good while we're here on the island. But what about when we get back home and go back to our lives? Aside from the issue with Hap, I've got my career in Eastport Bay, and you have your career... everywhere else. I mean, it'll be easy for you, but I'm different—especially when it comes to you."

I pushed up to one elbow, my head quirking to the side. "What's that supposed to mean? It'll be 'easy' for me?"

He rolled his head to the side to look at me, grasping a wet tendril of my hair and twirling it slowly around his finger. "Well, you know... the whole trail of broken hearts. I mean, chances are good I'll end up as just another platinum record on your wall."

For a moment I just stared at him in shock. My emotions progressed from confusion to irritation to flat out anger.

"Wilder Lowe, do you actually believe everything you read about me? You work with celebrities all the time, don't you? And you must have experienced some of the same garbage yourself back when you were a star athlete. Most of what people *think* they know about me isn't true. The rest is overblown. I've hardly even *dated* anyone, much less broken a bunch of hearts."

"Oh."

Beyond that single syllable, he seemed dumbstruck.

I pushed to my knees then stood, brushing sand from my legs. "I'm ready to go."

TWENTY
No-win Situation

Wilder

I wasn't sure if Jessica meant she was ready to go back to the house—or take the yacht and leave me stranded here on the island.

Based on the wake her digging strides left in the sand, it was the latter. I'd said the wrong thing... obviously.

Now that I thought about it, I of all people should have known better than to buy into the entertainment media's portrayal of "Jade" as a callous heartbreaker flitting from one guy to the next and coldly mining the intimate details of her relationships for songwriting fuel.

"I'm sorry." Grabbing the towels, I draped them over one arm and followed her.

"You're right. I remember how it was when I was playing football—the horrible stuff that was said on Twitter and the way the paparazzi press framed things to make something out of nothing. And then of course with my commander's court-martial and the shadow that cast on all of us publicly. I guess no one really knows what's going on in someone's life except the people who were there."

She stopped and turned to face me. "Exactly."

"Please accept my apology. That was totally out of line."

The anger drained from her eyes. It was replaced with something that looked like concern.

"That must have been so hard, that whole scandal and trial. And you've never said a thing about it—to the press or even to Hap."

A shot of white-hot pain pierced my heart. It was followed by the same dull ache that haunted me whenever I thought of the incident and its ugly aftermath.

My commanding officer had once been a personal hero of mine. A veteran of five combat zone deployments, he'd been a role model to all the younger SEALs.

But my fellow SEAL team members and I had seen our commander change over time. He'd become a rogue operator, making unwise decisions and leading the men under his charge into unnecessarily risky situations, sometimes violating orders and U.S. military rules and practices.

But that wasn't the worst of it by far. During our last mission, the commander had committed heinous acts of unnecessary violence against innocent civilians in the village where we were stationed.

We'd all seen him fire a sniper rifle into a shopping area filled with women and children, beat an elderly man who could barely walk, and then there was what he'd done to the teenaged girl—the *fourteen-year-old* teenaged girl.

He'd ordered us all to keep our mouths shut about it. Though I was sure it had devastated them all as much as it had me, I and every member of the team had broken the group's code of silence and testified against our chief in a military trial.

It had been a no-win situation with no good choices—but there had been only one choice that would allow me to live with myself.

I looked away from Jessica and continued walking, trying

to tamp down the flood of shame and anger those memories always triggered.

"I try not to think about it. It's in the past now anyway."

She refused to drop it, persisting with her soft eyes and sympathetic tone. "I hated the way you all got dragged through the mud. And then your commander lied about you. I knew you couldn't have had anything to do with it, but you never defended yourself publicly—even when your commander accused you of being a traitor to him and your country."

"Yeah well, the Trident badge is supposed to be a symbol of honor and uncompromising integrity," I said. "We took an oath to defend those who couldn't defend themselves, to serve with honor on and off the battlefield. Just because *he* broke it, that didn't mean I was going to. It was the toughest decision of my life to testify against him. It still bothers me sometimes."

She nodded. "Is *that* why you're so obsessed with being seen as 'loyal?' And with staying out of the spotlight?"

"I'm not 'obsessed.' I don't want to talk about this anymore." I opened the door to the house and went straight to the kitchen, getting a glass of water I didn't really want.

Jessica picked up her discarded sundress from the floor and followed me into the kitchen. "Wilder, you have nothing to be ashamed of and nothing to prove to anyone. You're a hero—for what you did as a SEAL and for what you did when you *left* the military. And now... you've provided jobs for your former team members, you keep people safe."

Softly she added, "You're keeping *me* safe."

As close as I'd felt to Jessica a few minutes earlier, now I found myself shutting down, withdrawing.

Instead of making me feel better, her words made me feel worse. I'd broken every rule of personal protection with her, stomped on every guideline. Perhaps worst of all, I'd violated Hap's trust in me.

In spite of what I'd just said to her, I *did* have a thing about loyalty. While in general it was a positive quality, even good things could be taken to an unhealthy extreme.

And now that I thought about it, I *was* obsessive about my privacy. I'd never liked fame, even the small amount I'd had back when I played college football on a championship team.

Infamy was a thousand times worse. I'd seen enough courthouse photos and unflattering headlines about myself and my disgraced SEAL brothers to last a lifetime.

These days I sought to be as invisible as possible, flying under the radar, treasuring my anonymity and using my past negative experiences with the tabloid press to help me advise celebrity clients on protecting and preserving their own privacy.

Even if Hap *didn't* murder me when we got back home—and that was a definite possibility—it wasn't like Jessica and I could make a life together.

Cos-playing *Blue Lagoon* a thousand miles from civilization was one thing—real life was another.

The fact was, she lived hers in the spotlight—and liked it that way.

Not only would it make me supremely uncomfortable to be followed and photographed and written about and speculated about on social media, but my past and my stained reputation would drag *her* down eventually.

She was just too caught up in her childhood crush on me to consider that right now. And I'd gotten too caught up in the incredible physical chemistry we shared.

Damn. What an idiot. I was supposed to be the *responsible* one. I was supposed to protect her, not romance her.

It had been weak and foolish of me to give into temptation and kiss her and touch her like I had tonight. I had to put a stop to this thing before it got any further out of hand.

"Look, you think you understand me, but you don't, okay? You don't know me at all," I said.

She flinched as if I'd taken a swing at her. "That's not true. Why are you pushing me away?"

"It is true. Before we came here, we hadn't talked in, what? Twelve, thirteen years? We're not a couple of happy little honeymooners off on some tropical getaway. This isn't Hollywood, a 'very special episode of *Just Jade*.' This is my job. And you're my best friend's little sister. You're a client. That's it."

Jessica looked unimpressed by my declaration. "Oh really? Do you give oral sex to all your clients? No wonder your security firm is so successful."

My brows lowered. "That was a mistake. It won't be repeated."

"Well at least *that* much is true," she said and spun on her heel, walking away toward the bedroom. A few seconds later, I heard the door slam and the shower turn on.

I went to the outdoor shower to cool off and to put as much distance between myself and the personification of temptation as possible.

But it was a small island.

Several oceans' distance wouldn't keep me from wanting her, not now that I'd gotten a taste of the forbidden fruit.

TWENTY-ONE

You're the Boss

Wilder

I woke just before dawn to powerful waves rocking my bed side to side.

I'd elected to spend the night on the yacht. Just like the house, it was equipped with radar equipment that would alert me if any watercraft approached the island or if the airspace overhead was violated.

Though I was farther away from Jessica in case of emergency, it was clear *I* was the biggest danger to her on the island.

It was better for both of us if I kept my distance.

Sitting up, I looked out the porthole. The water around the yacht was white-capping. Not good.

I'd been so caught up in Jessica yesterday, I hadn't checked the weather reports and doppler—another fail.

Checking it now, I saw the reason for the choppy waters. An enormous storm was approaching the island. It looked to be about an hour away.

Time to batten down the hatches—literally. I threw on some clothes and secured the yacht to the dock as well as possible then ran for the house.

By the time I reached it, the rain had started.

I wasn't worried about our safety. The house had weathered quite a few tropical storms since I'd built it.

Of course, none had been as large as this one looked. It wasn't a hurricane—yet—but it was on its way to becoming one, and it was certainly capable of producing damaging winds. In order to maximize the view, I'd used a *lot* of glass in constructing the waterfront home.

That was why I'd also had a storm shelter built. With the windspeeds that were heading our way, it would be the safest place for us during the storm.

Nothing like a palm tree sailing through your window to ruin your morning.

First I brushed my teeth, then I went to knock on the door of Jessica's room.

No response. I knocked again.

"Hey, you up? You awake, Jessica?"

Still nothing.

Feeling like I had no choice, I opened the door, girding myself to find her sleeping naked and vowing to be unaffected by the sight.

The room was empty. The bed had been made, and Jessica was nowhere in sight. I went to the open bathroom door and looked in. It was empty as well.

Where was she?

Our conversation had been spinning through my head all through the night and this morning. She'd shown compassion and understanding over my unfortunate brush with fame *after* I'd basically accused her of being a maneater.

And then I'd doubled down on my rudeness and idiocy by basically telling her she meant nothing to me.

Bottom line, I owed her an apology—big time.

But first, I had to get her to safety before that storm hit.

Moving through the house, I checked each room, looking for her. Where the hell could she be? My heart rate gained speed as I failed to find her in her usual spots.

Oh God, she hadn't decided to go for a hike or something, had she?

Surely she wouldn't attempt to climb to the summit or go to the waterfall alone?

Noticing the slider from the living room to the ocean-front balcony was slightly ajar, I sprinted to the glass door and pushed back the curtain—and let out a sigh of relief.

A candle burned on a low table. Curled up in a lounge chair beside it, Jessica was staring out at the approaching storm clouds, her pretty face in profile.

I leaned through the opening. "Hey."

Jessica turned, and I spotted the shiny tracks of recent tears in the weak morning light.

Awesome. You made the girl cry. Way to go. A giant hand squeezed my heart.

Pushing the door wider on its track, I stepped out onto the balcony, the warm ocean-scented breeze stirring my hair and sinking into my t-shirt.

"Hey." Jessica shifted to face me, making a quick swipe at her cheek with one hand. "Looks like a storm's coming."

I nodded. "A big one. We need to get down to the storm shelter before it hits. I'd say we've got about twenty minutes."

"The storm shelter? Is it that bad?"

"Could be. We'll be safe there though. I'm going to gather some food and other supplies. You should grab whatever you think you might need. Your pillow, some warmer clothes maybe, in case it cools off drastically."

She stood, hurrying into the house. "Okay. Where's the shelter?"

"It's built into the hillside here. The access is through the basement. I've got some things set up down there already—emergency rations, first aid kit, lanterns, a radio. But you should bring some things to make you comfortable and whatever you wouldn't be able to replace, you know, just in case the worst happens."

Jessica looked slightly alarmed. "I'll grab my guitar and my writing notebooks. Want me to get anything for you while you gather the food and stuff?"

"Nah, I'll stop by my office first and grab my briefcase." I patted my side. "I've got the satphone on me already. I'm used to gearing up on a moment's notice and moving fast when the situation calls for it."

"I'm sure," she said, and then she went to her room to gather her things.

We met back again a few minutes later in the kitchen. Jessica bore a slight resemblance to a little girl on her way to a slumber party, holding her blanket and a pillow, a small bag in tow as well as her beloved guitar.

"Too bad we can't bring the baby grand," she said. "I hope it doesn't get damaged."

"If it does, it's replaceable." I held up a thermos. "I found the coffee you made—thanks."

She nodded. "Sure, no problem. If I'd known this was going to happen, I'd have made some breakfast for you, too. I wasn't sure where you were. You weren't here when I got up this morning."

"Yeah, I, uh, slept on the boat."

"Oh." Jessica looked away at the window and then down.

Clearly our conversation from last night was still on her mind as well. The awkwardness between us was as thick as refrigerated peanut butter.

Well, we'd have an extended opportunity to clear the air. The storm was expected to last all day and through the night.

"Got everything?" I asked. When she nodded, I said, "Okay let's go."

She followed me down the stairs and through a short tunnel, up another set of steps, and into the storm shelter set into the stony hillside.

When I opened the door for her and she stepped inside, she gasped. "Oh. When you said storm shelter, I thought it would be some tiny little bunker with no headroom and a couple of folding chairs or something."

I grinned widely. "Big storms suck—that doesn't mean your storm shelter has to."

My storm shelter was more on the luxury side of things. The ceiling clearance was high enough that I didn't feel claustrophobic, even at six-foot-five.

Though it wasn't large, the single room shelter contained a kitchenette, a small dining area, and a daybed that served as both a couch for daytime and an extra-long twin-sized bed for night.

Unfortunately, there was only one of those. Like I said, I'd never planned on bringing anyone here, and it was plenty big enough for me to sleep on alone a night or two.

As Jessica would be sleeping in it tonight, it looked like another night of bunking on the floor for me.

She walked around the space, exploring. "There's a toilet," she said with obvious glee as she peeked behind the only door in the room.

"There is. And a shower. And power—for now. Let's hope that lasts. If not, that's what the battery-powered radio and lanterns are for."

Opening one of the small cabinets, I took out two coffee mugs and filled them from the thermos. Jessica took the one I offered her and went to sit on the daybed.

"Can I sit?" I gestured toward the other end of it.

She nodded, "Of course. It's your bed. It's your storm shelter."

Then in a surlier tone, she added, "I'm just a client."

I took a seat, leaning forward and resting my elbows on my knees.

It was easier to stare at the floor, but I forced myself to look at her.

"About that... I'm sorry. For what I said and the *way* I said it. It wasn't even true. You were never just a client, obviously. And I've always seen you as more than my best friend's little sister. I've always seen *you,* Jess."

I paused. "You see me too... for who I really am. I think that's why I freaked out on you last night. It scared me to realize how easily you could read me. I felt sort of like a cornered animal."

"Did you forget I've known you as long as you've known me?" she asked softly. "I'm sure you didn't realize it back then, but I paid close attention to you. I watched and listened, even when we were kids. I *do* know you, Wilder. I know you're a good man—you *are* loyal, almost to a fault. So you don't have to keep proving it over and over again. The people who know and love you..."

Here she stopped and swallowed. "... the people closest to you already know who you are. I've learned that's all that matters. If you worry about what the rest of the world thinks, you'll drive yourself crazy."

"You're right. I just..."

I looked down, took a breath, then met her eyes again. "I've struggled with it over the years. I left my football teammates to join the military. Then I was forced out of that before I was ready because of what my commanding officer did. It just hurts when I've been trying my best to be a loyal person to be accused of the opposite."

"I know."

Jessica got up and pulled something from her pocket. She came to sit right next to me, taking my hand and pressing something into my palm.

My notebook.

"*This*—is who you are. This is the Wilder Lowe I know. You left it on the piano last night. I didn't read anymore of it, by the way."

"It's okay if you did."

She gave me a guilty grin, holding up a hand with her thumb and forefinger spread a half-inch apart.

"Okay, good because I *might* have peeked just a little—just a couple of pages. I promise."

Sliding a hand around my nape, she massaged it. "One thing fame and this crazy entertainment business has taught me is the importance of really knowing yourself and trusting that who you are deep inside is *okay*. It's enough—even when people question what you do and say and print unflattering things about you, lies about you. Especially then."

She shrugged and scooted back on the daybed, leaning against the wall behind it.

"I'm sure when I don't show up for Coachella, they'll start saying I'm in rehab or had a nervous breakdown or something, but you know what? I don't *care*. I know the truth. I'd rather be here with you anyway."

I turned my head to meet her eyes again.

"How the fuck am I supposed to resist you?" I whispered.

"You're not." She laughed softly. "I told you to *stop* doing that."

For a minute I sat frozen as an internal battle raged inside. Was it worth it?

Worth the furious reaction I'd no doubt get from my best friend when Hap found out about this new development between his sister and me?

Worth the inevitable publicity storm when the entertainment media found out about the new man in Jade's life?

Jessica maintained our intense eye contact, looking at me with a secret smile that was both an invitation and a challenge.

"You're the boss," I whispered, then I reached over and pulled her down onto the bed with me. "And I know *exactly* who I am deep inside—yours. I'm yours Jessica, for as long as you want me."

TWENTY-TWO

Worth the Wait

Jessica

Now that Wilder had made up his mind, he was *serious* about it.

He rolled on top of me, pinning me with his body, touching and kissing me in a sort of sensual frenzy that had my head spinning and my body saying *Hooyah*.

It felt amazing, but he was also *really* heavy. Wilder was nearly three hundred pounds of muscle and bone, and while I wasn't a tiny woman, I was no Navy SEAL either.

He must have realized he was crushing me at about the same time I was trying to get his attention, because he did a pushup over me—at the *exact* moment I pushed on his side.

In a sudden, shocking motion, Wilder went right over the edge of the bed.

I scrambled to my knees, looking over the edge of it. "Oh my God, I'm so sorry. Are you okay?"

He reached up and rubbed the side of his forehead. "*Fuck.* You literally threw me out of bed. Was that payback for last night?"

I could tell by his tone of voice he was kidding. But I still felt terrible. And when he moved his hand, there was blood on it.

I slid off the bed, crouching beside him. "Oh no. You're hurt. What did you hit your head on? The floor?"

He looked a little embarrassed. "I think maybe it hit one of the metal latches on your guitar case. I hope I didn't break it."

Sure enough, the guitar case that had been leaning against the daybed was flat on the ground.

"I don't care about that," I said. "Let me see your head."

He swiveled it away from me and batted at my hand. "It's fine. Just a scratch."

I grabbed his hand out of the air and squeezed it. "We're on a remote island during a tropical storm. I am not going to let you get an infection. Now let me see it."

Finally, Wilder relented and let me examine him, sighing and rolling his eyes the whole time.

He got the most adorable little forehead crease whenever he looked at me like I was nuts. I was absolutely crazy about that little wrinkle, and I didn't want anything bad to happen to it—ever.

The injury was actually to the side of his forehead above the temple. He was right, it wasn't much more than a scratch.

But scratches could get infected. We were nowhere near any modern medical facilities.

The storm shelter seemed perfectly sanitary, but who knew where that guitar case had been? Airports. Tour buses. Stages all over the world.

And the latch was metal.

"Are you up to date on your tetanus shots?" I quizzed him.

"Yes ma'am, Nurse Jessica," he said. "But if it'll make you feel better, I'll roll over and let you give me a booster."

"You're a pervert."

"Yes, and you love it."

I got up and started rummaging through the cabinets. "Where is the first aid kit?"

"In the bathroom on the shelf."

I found the kit and looked through it, locating some wound wash, a bandage, and some antibacterial ointment. There were some unexpected items as well.

It was an exceptionally *well-appointed* kit.

Returning to the main room, I ordered Wilder to get back on the bed and lie down, which he did with a smile.

I climbed on top of him and straddled his waist, busying myself with cleaning the cut and applying ointment to the bandage.

Meanwhile, Wilder was rather busy himself. He slid his hands beneath my dress and caressed my thighs and bottom.

"I think you *like* this playing nurse thing," Wilder murmured. "I think I might have to get you a sexy little nurse costume for Halloween."

"You'd like that wouldn't you?"

"Yes. I would," he said. "And you'd like what I'll do to you when I take it off of you."

When I leaned forward to apply the bandage to his forehead, Wilder shifted one hand to my breast, causing my breath to catch.

He caressed me through the dress then lifted his head to kiss the tip of it, wetting the thin fabric with his mouth and making me squirm on top of him.

The hand that was on my thigh moved to my bottom, and he pulled me forward until my center rested directly on top of his erection.

A hiss of satisfaction escaped Wilder's lips.

"You feel so fucking good on me. So hot and wet."

He tugged the sundress aside and swirled his tongue over my budded nipple. I groaned and ground my clit against his hard shaft.

Letting out a groan of his own, Wilder said, "This is how we're going to have to do it, I think... so I don't crush you."

Gripping my hips in his large hands, he guided me up and down the length of him in a slow, erotic, fully clothed slide.

Fireworks ignited in my core and spread throughout my body as he continued to urge the front of me against him while nipping, lapping, and sucking at my breasts.

"Oh my God, I think I'm going to come just like this," I said in half-surprise, half-awe.

"Yes, hummingbird. I want you to. Come for me. Come right on my cock with your beautiful tits in my mouth."

That was an invitation I found impossible to refuse. Friction turned into frenzy, and I rocked against him, the delicious slide aided by his gentle but oh so strong hands.

Sensation built on sensation, sparks forming behind my eyes and alighting on my skin.

Bracing my palms against his shoulders, I sat upright and clamped his hips between my knees and tipping my head back with my mouth open in a silent scream.

It didn't stay silent.

In fact, I was so loud it was probably a good thing we were underground.

Because the Coast Guard might *actually* have been able to pick that one up from U.S. waters.

I collapsed onto Wilder, pressing my face into his neck and humming all over just like the little bird he nicknamed me for.

"Oh fuck, sweetheart, that was amazing." He ran his hands up and down my back, over my shoulders, beneath my bottom.

"You were so beautiful, going wild on top of me like that. I would give anything to be able to sink my cock inside you right now."

Lying limp against his chest, I smiled. "Anything?"

Wilder plunged both hands into my hair, kissing the top

of my head before dropping his back to the bed again. "Anything in the world."

Beneath me, his body was nearly vibrating with pent-up sexual energy. His legs were so tense they felt like bundles of steel cables.

Gripping his biceps, I pushed myself back up again and leaned backward, plucking something off the bedspread behind me.

I turned back to him, holding it in my closed fist.

"Guess what *else* I found in the emergency first aid kit?"

Opening my hand, I waggled the sealed condom package in front of his face, wearing a triumphant grin.

"Ta da!"

Wilder's jaw fell open and he grabbed the small package, studying it as if it were a gold nugget unearthed from a mine that had supposedly tapped out years ago.

"Are you kidding me? One of my guys at Viridian must have packed that in there, thinking he was being funny."

"Or practical," I said. "This *is* sort of an emergency."

"Oh really? And did you find any 'emergency lube?'"

Wilder gave me a sexy grin that qualified as a lubricant all on its own.

"We will *not* be needing any of that," I informed him. "You had me wet at 'I'm sorry.'"

He growled and reached up, pulling me down on top of him for a tantalizing kiss.

"Remind me to apologize more often."

"Well, we only have one condom, so you'd better not screw up again," I teased.

"I'll have more air-dropped tomorrow after the storm," he promised before kissing me hard again.

I pulled back. "Really? You can do that?"

"If necessary. We'll worry about that tomorrow. Right now, let's open the one we have—even my first phase instructors in SEALs training didn't dole out torture like this... and they were fucking sadists."

Crawling off of Wilder so we could both undress, I ripped open the foil packet—carefully—and rolled the condom onto him.

Thankfully, whoever put it in the first aid kit selected the extra-large variety because Wilder was built to scale—size-matched all over.

Puberty hadn't been *good* to him—it had been extra *extra* good.

In fact, I was getting a little scared.

Once it was on, he flipped me over and began another tender assault of insatiable kisses.

Working his way down my body, he kissed and nibbled and licked until excitement vibrated through every part of me and I was ready for anything and everything he could possibly throw my way.

I didn't care if there was a condom or no condom, if he was the size of a golf pencil or a Pringles can—I had to have him inside of me.

He nudged at my entrance, careful not to go too fast.

Any worries I had disappeared as he pushed inside. I was so turned on there was no pain at all, only tightness and an almost incandescent sense of joy that it was finally happening.

And Wilder... well he looked like he might be having an out of body experience.

I loved the way his eyelids went heavy and the hazel irises beneath them glazed over with pleasure.

Then his eyes closed completely, and he dropped his damp forehead to my shoulder.

"So good," he panted. "You feel so good, I... I think we're gonna need that air-drop, hummingbird. Cause there's no way this is gonna last long."

The passionate confession touched my heart, and I kissed

his neck, the top of his chest, anything I could reach. Petting his back, I slid my hands lower to pull him more deeply into me.

"It's good for me, too... just like this," I assured him. "Just having you inside me is all I need."

However, the moment he started thrusting, I was right back in the game. The combination of his thickness pressing against the inside of me and his lean abdomen pressing against the outside had me on the verge of another orgasm within minutes.

"Don't go slow," I urged him. "Don't be careful."

That was all Wilder needed. His pace picked up, and he buried himself in me again and again, using his powerful thighs and hips to drive me to a shattering climax.

Then locking his lips with mine, he thrust upward once more and shuddered.

* * *

Making love with Wilder had been sweet, and surprising, exciting, and emotional. And absolutely worth the wait.

Afterward we lay tangled together, drowsily stroking each other and exchanging sleepy murmurs about the sound of the wind outside, the past we'd shared long ago, and the pleasure we'd shared moments ago.

And I reflected on the night he burst into my closet to find me naked and terrified, realizing I was actually grateful to that psycho stalker, whoever and wherever he was.

It might have been stupid, but I hoped he'd manage to elude the police for at least a little while longer.

Because hidden away on a remote island, cuddling in a storm shelter in a much-too-small bed with Wilder Lowe was absolute paradise.

Tracing the colorful tattoo on his shoulder, I asked,

"When did you get your tattoos? You didn't have any in high school."

He kept his eyes closed as he answered, drawing lazy circles on my back with his fingers.

"In the Navy. My buddy Gray did them. He's a hell of an artist—designed all our tattoos— our whole team got them."

"What does the owl on your back mean?"

"Owls symbolize wisdom and endurance," he said. "And some cultures also believe owls are harbingers of death. Seemed appropriate."

"And this?" I caressed the skull design that covered his entire right shoulder and upper arm.

He chuckled. "Well, obviously skulls symbolize death. Generally people get skull tattoos to show they have no fear of death."

"Or snakes apparently. " I wrinkled my nose. "Your skull is *eating* one."

He laughed again. "Yeah, well, the rattlesnake stands for hidden evil and danger. Rooting that out and crushing it is worth risking death."

I sighed against his pec muscle. "I'm glad you're not putting your life on the line everyday anymore. I can't stand the thought of anything happening to you."

His hand on my back moved in a soothing rub and then a little pat. "Nothing's going to happen to me. And nothing's going to happen to you, either. Not while I'm around."

After a while, Wilder fell asleep, but I tried my best not to. I lay there soaking in the sight and smell and feel of him, trying to memorize every detail of this night and praying there'd be countless more like it.

At some point I must have dozed off because I was awakened by the bleating of the satphone.

The foreign sound caused my heart to leap into my throat and Wilder to wake instantly from a dead sleep.

One of his arms wrapped around me. The other shot out and brought the wretched device to his ear.

"Lowe here. What's going on?"

I curled against Wilder's side, nuzzling into his warm skin while inside I made a silent plea.

Not yet. Please not yet.

TWENTY-THREE
Jade's List

Jessica

"That's great news." Wilder had been scribbling furiously on a notepad since about thirty seconds after picking up the call.

"They're sure it's the right guy?" he asked. "Okay, yeah. Sounds good. Yeah, what a relief."

With every exclamation from his mouth, my heart sank farther. It was obvious the police had found my stalker.

Which meant we'd be leaving the island. It looked like I'd make it home in time to perform at Coachella after all. And make my scheduled appearance on the Late Show. And at the concert in Venice as well.

All of that was good news, or it should have been. In spite of all my bellyaching about being "bored" and "stuck" on the island," the events of the past two days had me wishing Wilder and I could stay here forever.

Especially as skittish as he obviously was about our new relationship. I took heart in the fact that at least I *knew* I was no longer alone in this thing—he *did* want me the way I wanted him.

At least I *hoped* he was through holding me at arm's length and keeping things "professional." I never wanted to go back to the way things used to be. I wanted to be with him all the time and let the whole world know he was mine.

Would it bother my fans if every song I wrote from here on out was called, "Wilder?"

Ending the call, he smiled at me. "Ready to go home?"

"Yes," I lied. "So where did they find him? Who is it?"

"They followed up on some weird posts on social media, found evidence the guy had basically been following you around the country on your tour—even to some of the international shows."

"I have lots of fans who do that, though."

"Well, apparently he went a few thousand miles past fandom. They searched his apartment and found some creepy cut and paste photos starring you and him in... how shall I put this... fantasy scenarios—and I don't mean dressed as characters from Game of Thrones."

A surge of bile rushed up my esophagus, leaving an acrid taste in my mouth. "Gross. Okay well, at least they caught him. I'm safe again, and we can go back to the 'real world.' I will miss it here, though."

"I thought you were going stir-crazy."

"Well, I was, but only because you and I weren't communicating. It was driving me mad to keep my feelings for you all bottled up. I wasn't tired of hiding physically as much as I was drained from hiding my emotions day after day. I don't ever want us to do that. I want things to be out in the open from now on."

A dark cloud passed over Wilder's face. "About that..."

"What?"

"I'm not sure we should go public—I mean, not right away."

"You ashamed to join 'Jade's list?'" I teased, though my question was more serious than I let on.

He didn't answer it directly. "I'm concerned about Hap's reaction for sure."

"Wait—you don't think he's going to be mad, do you?" I laughed. "I know he used to threaten you guys about staying away from his 'baby sister,' but he was kidding. Besides, we're all grown-ups now."

"Yeah, well I'm not sure he's actually grown out of his overprotective streak—not where you're concerned. And I don't think he was kidding. There's a very good chance he'll take out a hit on me—and he has the money to do it."

I moved close to him, wrapping my arms around his neck and smiling up into his handsome, worried face. "Hap loves you—nothing could ever change that."

"Well, I guess we'll find out. Maybe... if you wouldn't mind, could we just wait until after we get back from Coachella to tell him about us?"

My heart zinged with delight. "We? You're coming with me?"

"Is that okay? I know your record company only provides personal security when you're on tour for them. I want to make sure you're safe there."

His fierce protectiveness melted my heart. But then protecting people *was* his job. Was that all this was? We hadn't talked about any sort of lasting future together.

"Of course I want you to come," I said. "If it were up to me, I'd have you travel with me full-time. And yes, we can wait until afterward to tell people."

A micro-expression crossed his face, the hint of a wince. "Listen, as far as going public... I'm not sure we even have to *make* an announcement. It's no one else's business really. And I'm an expert at maintaining privacy—one of my specialties is helping my celebrity clients elude the paparazzi. When people see you and me together, they'll just assume I'm your new bodyguard. We should let them. We can probably keep this thing quiet for months—maybe years if we're careful."

"Uh huh." I turned away, folding a shirt and placing it in my suitcase. "You're probably right."

It all sounded so reasonable, so sane. So why had the last few minutes reawakened my fears and set them dancing on the grave of my newfound hope for us? *Could* our fledgling relationship survive the rigors of the real world?

It didn't help that Wilder wanted to keep our connection a secret. It was too much like what had happened when I was sixteen and he'd basically acted like our amazing first kiss had never happened.

In his determination to protect his friendship with Hap, he'd shoved me right back into the little sister zone and essentially removed himself from my life. Would that happen again when push came to shove?

If Wilder turned out to be just another frog I'd kissed, my heart would break.

Only time would tell.

At least we had a little more of that. The flight back to the States would take almost twenty-four hours, and we'd be in California for the Coachella festival for several days before returning to Eastport Bay.

As we left the gorgeous beach house and walked down the dock to the yacht together, I determined to make the most of it, to enjoy every minute I had with Wilder.

And to convince him we *were* meant to be, no matter what my fans—or my brother—might think of it.

TWENTY-FOUR

The Safest Place

Jessica

Indio, California, where the Coachella Valley Music Festival was held, was *hot,* even in April.

It was near Palm Springs, surrounded by desert. Which meant there was a considerable amount of dust in the air. Wilder and I both wore dust masks as we made our way around the polo fields that served as the concert venue.

Not only was it smart to protect my soon-to-be used vocal cords, the mask also provided some anonymity. I liked that more than I'd anticipated.

Being on the island away from the constant pressure of fan interaction had been good for me—healthy and refreshing in a way I didn't even know I'd needed. It wasn't easy to return to it in such an abrupt total immersion fashion.

Wilder kept a protective arm around me as we walked, using his considerable wingspan and the power of his other arm to keep the other festival goers from colliding with me.

"You okay?" he asked, ducking his head to speak close to my ear.

I nodded. "I'm great."

It was true. Tucked up against Wilder's solid ribcage, I'd never felt so safe in my life. Too bad he *couldn't* really go with me everywhere I went. But he had a business to run, and it wasn't like he was just going to drop everything else in his life to be with me.

As for my career, I couldn't even entertain the idea of stepping away from public life and staying home in Eastport Bay. I still owed my record label another album, which would have to be supported by tour dates and promotional stops.

The same issues that had prevented me from having any real, lasting relationships before still existed. Hopefully my newly forged connection with Wilder would be strong enough to withstand them all.

Once I'd safely reached the backstage area, I removed my mask. I was filled with the same nervous energy that always invaded my body before a performance. Tapping into it allowed me to transform myself from Jessica to Jade and give audiences the high energy shows they'd come to expect from me.

Smiling up at Wilder, I said, "Wish me luck?"

He dipped his head, matching my smile with a bone melting one of his own. "You don't need luck. You're amazing."

And then he kissed me. Long and oh-so-sweet, the kiss made me eager to get the performance over with and get back to him.

Opening my eyes, I took a breath and walked out of his arms onto the main stage.

It was my first time performing at the music festival, and the Coachella crowd lived up to the hype. I hoped they were having as good a time as I was. The desert sunset during my set was something I'd never forget.

It was dark by the time I sang my final number, a ballad

called *Let Down Your Hair.* I'd written it for Sullivan Reece's wedding, and it had become one of my biggest hits.

After the final notes, as the crowd cheered, I walked offstage to the left, the opposite side from where Wilder stood watching and clapping. I was planning to give it about a minute before returning to the stage for an encore—a high energy song that would hopefully leave the audience pumped.

Several members of the concert security staff complimented my performance while my wardrobe assistant Lila made an adjustment to my costume. I was about to step out from behind the large screen wall to take the stage again when one of the security guards leaned close to my ear.

"Ma'am there's been an accident. Please come with me."

"What do you mean? What happened?"

"It's your bodyguard. He fell from the stage while trying to take a photo of your performance."

My feet were already moving as I accompanied the man through the dark backstage area toward the stairs. "Is he okay? Did someone call an ambulance? How far did he fall?"

"I don't know ma'am. I was just sent to get you. I think he's still alive."

Oh no. The fact that was even in question flooded my mind with mind-scrambling fear. *Please don't let him be seriously hurt.*

Serious stage-falls weren't uncommon. I'd seen several over the years. They could result in broken bones, concussions, even death.

"Where are you going?" Lila called as I rushed past her.

"It's Wilder. He's hurt."

"But your encore..."

Lila's voice drifted away as the guard and I reached the bottom of the steps. He held my upper arm for support as I walked as quickly as possible in the high-heeled boots I'd worn for the show.

Behind the stage there was no waiting ambulance, only throngs of music lovers moving through the dark space from one stage to the next.

The guard pulled me into the swarm of people, walking quickly.

"Where are you taking me? Where's Wilder?"

Had they already transported him to the hospital? Was this man supposed to give me a ride there?

His grip on my arm tightened. "Just a little further, Jessica."

"Wait." I stopped walking, digging my sharp heels into the ground as a cold finger of dread trailed down my back.

Jessica?

It wasn't *impossible* that the concert staff might know my real name. But there was something familiar about the guard.

I hadn't gotten a good look at him due to the darkness but something about his voice...

"There's a police truck right over there. Can't they give me a ride?" I asked as panic over Wilder's well-being shifted into fear for my own safety.

"They're watching the VIP area. Do you want to see your handsome boyfriend or not?" The man sneered. "He might be dying."

Something was definitely wrong. I'd seen this man somewhere before.

Casting a glance back toward the rear of the stage I'd just left, I spotted a tall figure running from one side to the other, headed for the stairs.

"Is that... that's *Wilder*," I gasped. Having spent a shameful amount of time watching him—in person and on TV when he played football—I recognized the way he moved.

I whirled back to face the blond security guard, who now had my arm in a painful steel grip as he dragged me along with him.

"Who are you? What's going on here?"

He didn't answer but attempted to get a hand over my mouth. "Let's put this dust mask on you okay? Don't want you to ruin those golden pipes of yours."

I bit the man's hand then twisted my neck to shout behind me. "Wilder!" I screamed. "I'm here. Wilder! Help me!"

This time the guard did manage to clamp a hand over my mouth, muffling my shouts. But our struggle had drawn the attention of some of the people around us.

"Hey is that Jade?" a girl said.

The guard pulled my face against his shoulder. "Out of the way please. Concert security. Please clear a path or you're the next pothead who's going down. You ready for a pat-down?"

His threatening tone worked. The clearly inebriated—or otherwise impaired—music lovers backed away. One of them though, a super-thin, shirtless guy with shaggy dark hair and glassy eyes stared at me.

"I could swear that's Jade. She looks just like her." He raised his voice. "Hey, I think this guy's arresting Jade."

I heard some exclamations of surprise but couldn't see the crowd's reaction because my captor had picked up his pace and was now fully dragging me toward the perimeter of the festival grounds, where rows of vehicles were parked.

If I allowed him to get me into one of those, I had no doubt I'd never be seen again. I'd never see Wilder again.

Drawing my knee up, I turned and struck out with one of my heels. The sharp point of it made contact with the man's lower leg, and he yelped in pain as his grip loosened. I let my body go slack, dropping to the ground and breaking his hold entirely.

A large male body launched over me and crashed into the security guard, taking him down in a violent bone-crunching tackle.

The yelp turned into an agonized scream. It was cut off by the sound of several rapid-succession blows.

When I sat up, I saw Wilder on top of my kidnapper battering his face with a volley of punches. Several security guards and police officers arrived, guns drawn, one of them yelling into a radio attached to his shirt. Another pulled Wilder off the moaning man.

"What's going on here?" the cop yelled at Wilder.

I answered. "He just saved me. That guy was trying to abduct me, and he stopped him."

"Yeah, but Jade did a little girl-power judo move of her own first," the skinny, shirtless guy said with a laugh, holding up his phone. "I just Snapped a video of it."

"What's your Snap code?" someone else called out and several others pulled out their phones.

Apparently satisfied by my explanation, the police officer released his hold on Wilder, who immediately turned and moved toward me. He helped me to my feet and wrapped me in a hold so tight it was nearly crushing.

I managed to work my hands in between our bodies and pressed against his chest. "Honey, you're smothering me." I let out a weak laugh.

Wilder shifted his hands to my head, cradling it as he searched my face with frantic eyes. "Sorry—I was so scared. Are you okay? Did he hurt you?"

"No. I'm okay. I was calling for you. Did you hear me?"

"I heard you, hummingbird. I'd know that voice anywhere." His voice turned rusty, and his eyes filled with tears. "Thank God you're okay. I don't know what I would have done if—"

He stopped right there, electing to finish the thought with a kiss instead of words.

I sank into the wonderful warmth of it, the feel and scent and taste of Wilder—the safest place I'd ever known.

TWENTY-FIVE

Out of the Bag

Wilder

All around us cell phone cameras flashed.

Some part of me knew that wasn't a good thing, but I couldn't stop kissing Jessica. I'd come so close to losing her.

My heart was still thrashing in my chest, partially due to the mad dash to get to her and the fight with the guy who'd grabbed her and partially due to the thought of what could have happened to her if the man had succeeded in throwing her into one of the nearby cars.

This had been a close one, and I still wasn't sure how it had happened.

I'd watched her performance, nearly mesmerized by her incredible voice and stage presence. I was so proud of her, so happy for her that she'd achieved the success I always believed she deserved.

When the set ended, I'd watched her leave the stage on the opposite side, expecting like everyone else that she'd return for an encore. When she hadn't, I'd assumed she'd simply decided not to do one.

So I'd started making my way to her via the walkway

behind the main stage's enormous rear video wall. When I'd emerged in the other backstage wing, I'd taken one look at Jessica's wardrobe assistant and known something was very wrong.

The woman had stared at me like I was a ghost. Then her hands had come up to cover her mouth. "Oh no."

"What's the matter?" I'd demanded.

"She thought you were hurt. She went that way." She pointed toward the stairs at the rear stage exit. "She was with a security guard."

I hit the stairs at a dead run. There was only one reason Jessica would have thought I was injured.

Someone had lied to her—most likely the "security guard" who'd led her away.

How *could* I have let it happen? I'd let my own guard down, so concerned with allowing her to do her job without me hovering that I hadn't done *my* job—keeping her safe.

Drawing back a few inches and obviously just noticing all the cameras documenting our dramatic reunion scene, Jessica smiled up at me, clearly oblivious to the firestorm torching my heart and soul.

"Well, so much for holding off on telling people—I think the cat's out of the bag."

I gave a humorless laugh. It wouldn't be funny at all if Hap was on the internet tonight. No doubt the story of Jade's close call with a would-be kidnapper had already spread like wildfire—along with the accompanying photos of her rescue.

Well fuck. I'm going to have some explaining to do.

Aloud I said, "The most important thing is that you're okay."

And that was the truth. That was what I had to focus on, though self-recrimination threatened to swamp me.

"I love you, Wilder," Jessica said quietly.

The air left my lungs with a whoosh. Before I could

respond, the police officer and his partner were back, addressing Jessica.

"We've got an ambulance here for you ma'am. If you'll come this way..."

She tried to protest. "I'm okay, really."

"You should go," I said. "Get checked out. I'll feel better if you do. I need to speak to the officers and other security guards anyway, get some information on that scumbag lying in a puddle over there and figure out how he got close to you."

"Okay. You'll come to the hospital and pick me up afterward?"

"Of course. I'll be there soon. Don't leave without me."

"I won't."

"We'll take care of her sir," the young officer assured him. "She'll be at Desert Regional Medical Center."

"Okay thanks."

One more kiss and I watched Jessica climb into the back of the emergency vehicle with the two officers. Then I spoke with the other law enforcement members on site as well as a representative from the security company in charge of staffing the main stage.

I learned the festival organizers had stepped up security in recent years following the Route 91 Harvest Festival tragedy in Las Vegas, posting officers with rifles in high and low-profile observation areas in case of a lone shooter situation or terrorist act.

But scores of additional security personnel were needed to deal with things like traffic, ingress, egress, flow inside and outside the venue, check-ins, check-outs, credentialing, and searches of cars, bodies, and containers like purses and coolers.

There literally weren't enough available police officers in the city of Indio or the surrounding departments to cover it. So a large private security company as well as several smaller ones were brought in to make up the difference.

The blond assailant had been wearing the uniform of one of them. I wasn't sure at this point whether he'd stolen it or if he'd actually been hired by one of the companies.

An employee I interviewed told me about a cattle call interview in Long Beach where he'd been hired, along with several friends, after a quick background check.

They'd all been shuttled off to an orientation, and a few weeks later, here he was, sleeping in a tent, sweltering during the day, shivering through the night, and charged with protecting crowds of over a hundred-twenty-five-thousand people, including an astonishing number of celebrities.

Speaking with a police detective assigned to Jade's case, I said, "It's the perfect situation for an obsessed fan."

I also wanted a word with whomever had determined the man they'd arrested a few days ago was indeed the *same* stalker who'd broken into Jessica's houses. The lengths *this* guy had gone to in order to get close to her—and the desperation of abducting her while surrounded by a crowd of witnesses—made me wonder.

And he looked an awful lot like the security guard I'd found unconscious in the foyer of Jessica's Eastport Bay mansion. Correction—he *had* looked like that guy until I'd permanently altered his face. Now I doubted if the guy's own mother could I.D. him.

Before I could make the call, my phone rang with an incoming one. Lifting the device, I saw the name on the screen, closed my eyes, and exhaled.

Hap. *Fantastic.*

Though I would have loved to duck the call, I swiped the screen to answer. Jessica's brother had to be frantic for news about her.

"Hey. She's okay. She's at the hospital getting checked out, but she said she was uninjured, and she looked fine," I said.

Hap's voice sounded like a growl coming through the long-distance line.

"Good. Now that's out of the way, I have *another* question. When *exactly* were you planning to tell me you'd seduced my baby sister—while she was at her *most* vulnerable?"

TWENTY-SIX
Buy a Ticket

Jessica

Wilder was acting weird.

Not rude exactly, but not like he had been when we'd first left the island. At the hospital, he'd been all business. Now on the private flight home, he seemed reserved, a bit aloof.

Like he used to be.

He wasn't touching me. When I'd tried to kiss him, he'd gently evaded it, claiming to have a lot on his mind.

I hoped he didn't feel guilty over the almost-kidnapping. It wasn't his fault. Who in the world could have anticipated it happening during a concert in the middle of a crowd?

The man who'd done it was clearly insane, and you simply couldn't prepare for insanity.

While the police *had* arrested a dangerous stalker—it hadn't been the same man who'd broken into my Eastport Bay home the night Wilder had come to my rescue.

No, *that* man had gotten away with his crime and shown up later at Coachella to try to snatch me there.

His name was John Delacroix. Like the other stalker, he

had an obsession with me. Unlike the other man, Delacroix had access to me.

In his confession he said that while he hadn't been assigned to my home in Eastport Bay that night, he did work for my former security company and had been sent to the estate on occasion to fill in if one of the other guys was sick or had a conflict.

He knew the other guards and had easily fooled them when he'd stopped by with a kind offer of hot coffee on that chilly night.

He also *knew* security guards had extreme access to their celebrity clients. And not all security companies were as strict as Wilder's when it came to the interview process.

The kidnapper had worked in several security jobs over the years, moving around the country, and keeping his record spotless.

After I'd gone off the grid that night, he'd begun making plans to gain employment at one of the venues where he knew I was scheduled to perform.

Anyway, the guy was locked away now, and I was fine. I just wanted things to get back to normal—or what I *hoped* was the new normal, which was Wilder and me together and happy. We hadn't yet made any sort of formal declaration of coupledom, and he didn't seem exactly happy.

In the seat beside me he sat staring out the jet's window where wispy clouds glowed like shreds of cotton candy in the day's waning light.

"You okay?" I asked.

He blinked, as if resurfacing from some very deep thinking and turned toward me. "Yeah. You?"

I nodded, eager to reassure him. "I am. I'm completely fine. So I don't want you to beat yourself up. Everything's going to be okay."

He frowned. "Not too sure about *that.* You didn't hear him on the phone."

I blinked in confusion. "On the phone? You talked to the kidnapper?"

"What? No. To Hap. I was talking about Hap."

"Oh. What did he say?"

Wilder gave an unwilling shake of the head. "Never mind."

I touched his arm. "No, don't do that. Tell me. What did he say?"

He sniffed a laugh and scratched his face. "I probably shouldn't repeat it in front of a lady. Suffice it to say he is *not* happy with me."

"Is that what's got you in a funk—Hap reading you the 'my baby sister' riot act? Who cares? I don't. He'll get over it."

"I care, Jess. He's my best friend. I don't know if he's ever gonna forgive me."

"For what? Protecting me? Giving up weeks of your life to take me somewhere safe and then stopping the guy who was trying to drag me off and nearly beating him to death? Hap should be thanking you, not harassing you. What a bully."

"He's not being a bully. He loves you. He just wants what's best for you."

I placed a hand on his shoulder. "He loves you too, Wilder. And *you're* what's best for me."

"That's debatable," he muttered, turning away again.

The quiet words stopped my heart cold. "Why would you say that?"

Wilder's shoulders lifted and fell in a sullen shrug. "It's not the first time a girl's been hurt on my watch."

"You're talking about the situation in Iraq?"

He nodded, returning his gaze to the window. The flight must have been near its end because the view of clouds had given way to landscape below, the miniature homes and cars growing larger in perspective.

"Emotion got in the way that time, too. I was so loyal to my commanding officer, I had so much admiration and respect for him I didn't follow my instincts. I followed his orders and left him alone with her when I knew better—I *knew* better. I *let* that girl get hurt."

He pounded the arm rest. "I almost let *you* get hurt."

I stroked his tense forearm and the back of his hand. "I *wasn't* hurt. And there's nothing you could have done to prevent what happened—he was hired as a security guard after a background check. He had no record. And you stopped him in time. All's well that ends well, right?"

I didn't like the determined set of Wilder's jaw or the sound of his *hmmph* response. Maybe changing the subject would help.

"When I spoke to Hap, all he did was ask about how I was feeling. What did he say to you?"

"He asked how I could seduce you when you were at your most vulnerable." Wilder slid his eyes over to meet mine again.

I barked a short, sharp laugh. "That's ridiculous. I'm not sixteen. I'm a grown woman. And if anything, I was the aggressor. What did you tell him?"

"The truth. That I'd never take advantage of you. That I have too much respect for you to treat you like a one-night stand or a casual fu—relationship."

My eyebrows shot up. "And what did he say?"

Wilder didn't answer, just looked at me with a bleak expression.

"What, are you afraid it might scar my tender ears?"

Still nothing. His lack of response was starting to make me nervous.

"Look, when we get home, we'll talk to him," I said. "I'll tell him that like it or not, we're together now, so he'll just have to get used to it."

Still no response. *Uh oh.* "We are, aren't we? Together?"

Wilder's jaw hardened even further, and his brows dropped low over his eyes, which looked very dark at the moment. "I'm not sure that's... the best thing for everyone involved."

My heart lurched. "Oh no—don't you do this to me again, Wilder Lowe. When we were young and you kissed me, I was too inexperienced to know whether you meant it or not. But what happened between us on the island—and the way you kissed me after the concert when you rescued me—you *meant* that. You love me just like I love you. I know you do."

Though his eyes were screaming *Yes I do*, Wilder's mouth stayed firmly shut.

Tears collected behind my own eyes while a hard lump formed in my throat.

"I'm leaving Eastport Bay for Venice in a week to perform at the Mad Music festival. Will you be with me... or not?"

His face remained an unemotional mask.

"Anthony will keep you safe while you're in Eastport Bay. First thing tomorrow morning I'll start looking into a full-time bodyguard to travel with you to Italy and wherever you go after that. I've already proved I'm not equal to the task."

I could hardly believe my ears. But then why should I be shocked? It was just more of the same indifference he'd shown me all our lives.

I'd been a fool to think a few weeks alone together would change things.

The tears spilled over, and I unbuckled my seat belt, standing to move to the opposite side of the jet's cabin.

"Yes. You have. And that won't be necessary. You're fired. I'll hire my own security."

He shot me a pleading look. "Jessica..."

"I'm serious Wilder. I can't take it anymore. I've wasted

too much of my life wanting you, and it's obvious I need to stop. So please... don't call me. Don't text 'just to check up' on me. Don't drop by. I don't ever want to see your face again. If you want to see me... you can buy a ticket like everyone else."

TWENTY-SEVEN
Distraction

Wilder

I flung the empty gel pen across my office. It struck the large dry erase board with a crack and a metallic ping before falling to the floor in two pieces.

Roughly yanking open my desk drawer, I rummaged through it for a fresh pen, slamming my hand on the desktop when I failed to locate one. I jammed my thumb against the intercom button connecting me to my secretary.

"What do I have to do to get a working pen around here?" I barked.

Kiara responded immediately. "I'll get some from the supply closet and be right in."

Two minutes later, Gray came into my office with a handful of writing instruments.

He fanned them out like a deck of cards. "One of every shade," he said.

Taking in my scowl, he dropped his own smile and laid the pens on the desk. "What's going on, boss?"

"Nothing. I'm just trying to get this paperwork done, and I can't find a fucking pen that works, that's all."

"Okay well, I get that. It's just..." Gray rubbed his face, clearly reluctant to continue.

"What?" I growled.

"It's not like you to get upset over the small things, you know? You haven't been acting like yourself since you got back. Kiara asked me to bring you the pens because she was literally afraid to come in here. She's convinced you're about to fire her."

He paused. "Look, I know Jessica was scheduled to fly out to Venice this morning. Want to talk about it?"

"There's nothing to talk about. It's over. I'm fine. I just want to get back to life as usual."

Gray nodded slowly and backed toward the door as I returned my focus to the papers in front of me. "Okay then. If you change your mind... you know where to find me."

When he reached the door, Gray didn't leave but paused in the opening. "I'll just say one more thing. The life you had before? It wasn't all that hot."

My head whipped up. "What's that supposed to mean?"

Gray held his hands out in front of him in a don't-shoot-me gesture. "I'm just sayin'... your 'life as usual' kinda sucked. Yeah, you had a successful business and plenty of money, but other than a few friends like me and Hap and Sully Reece, you had no personal life. The job's not gonna keep you warm at night and give you children and keep you company in your old age. A *job* doesn't make life worth living."

"I don't see you settling down and getting married," I snarled.

"Hey, I'm trying. It's not easy to find the right girl. The problem with you is—you already have. You just won't man up and be with her. If you ask me, you ought to get on a plane and get yourself out to Italy before she gives up on you altogether."

Somehow my glare didn't turn my friend into a column of ash.

"I *didn't* ask you. Don't you have a project to take care of? Or have you decided to go into full-time couples therapy?"

Gray snickered and left the room, shutting the door behind him and leaving me alone in the quiet office.

It was *too* quiet. Quiet was bad. Quiet left space for thinking, and there was apparently only one thing I was capable of thinking about anymore.

My brain aired the Jessica Bailey show twenty-four-seven —and not the kids TV program I'd secretly recorded and watched every episode of when she'd starred in it years ago. The reel playing in my head was comprised of all the real-life moments we'd shared together—the good, the bad, the frightening, and the beautiful.

If things were different, it could have been a preview of a full life together.

She'd said she loved me. But it wasn't possible for us. First, my oldest friend probably hated me because I'd slept with his little sister.

Second, though Jessica was worth tolerating a life in the spotlight, I wasn't too sure I was worthy of *her*. I'd failed her just like I'd failed that village girl.

Only this time everyone, including Jessica, considered me a hero. It was only stupid luck she hadn't ended up being abducted.

Intending to find some music to drown out the morose thoughts, I pulled my phone from my pocket. When I glanced at the screen, I saw I'd missed a text from Bree Steele.

Bree: You back in town? Would love to get together. Anytime.

Ah, distraction, my old friend. I could text Bree back, make plans, maybe even take Gray's advice and actually let a woman into my heart.

An image of Jessica, smiling at me with the turquoise waves of my island paradise behind her, filled my mind's eye. And a swell of sweet, painful emotion filled my entire body.

Who was I kidding? There was *already* a woman in my heart.

Somehow Jessica had picked the lock, moved in, and furnished every room in her own personal style. No one else would ever fit.

All I wanted was to be with her. It was driving me crazy to know that she was halfway across the world by now.

Fuck. I wished I'd gotten on that plane with her.

I wanted to stay with her all the time, wherever she was, to protect her, to *love* her... till death did us part.

I did not return Bree's text.

Instead, I swiped the screen to bring up Hap's name.

I hadn't spoken to my lifelong friend since I'd been home. Having no good defense for what I'd done—other than *I love her*—I'd decided to let Jessica tell Hap whatever she wanted to about our relationship and allow some time to pass before I attempted to mend fences.

Maybe one day Hap's anger would cool and he'd forgive me. Maybe *today* was that day.

After all, Jessica had been willing to defy the world, to risk her heart and risk angering her brother to be with me. People always talked about my courage, but hers put mine to shame.

My finger trembling, I tapped the call button.

"Wilder. I wondered when I'd be hearing from you."

"I wasn't sure you'd want to."

There was a pause. "I'd rather talk in person. You free for lunch? Want to meet me at Nooky's?"

My pulse spiked with adrenaline and shock. "Give me fifteen minutes."

TWENTY-EIGHT
Seven Ways to Sunday

Wilder

I stepped into Nooky's, the bell over the door signaling my entrance.

The all-day-all-night diner on Eastport Bay's waterfront main street was famous for two things—its cheeky slogan, "Come and Get it All Night Long," and its pie.

Though Nooky's served all kinds of food, there were never fewer than ten varieties of pie listed on the chalkboard wall menu.

The railcar-shaped diner's retro décor included red-and-white checkered floor tiles, red laminate tabletops, and a long, chrome-topped counter with barstools.

As it had been in business since the '50's, the diner's walls were a virtual time capsule. They were covered with photos of Eastport Bay's history as well as pieces of sports memorabilia recalling the triumphs of local teams like the Patriots, Celtics, and Red Sox—even a signed photo of my friend Sullivan Reece, who was a former world heavyweight boxing champ and Eastport Bay resident.

Lunchtime was always busy here, and today was no exception. About three-quarters of the tables contained lunch patrons. Several more came in behind me, asking to be seated.

Hap was already there seated in a booth. He stood when he spotted me. And smiled.

That was a surprise. When I reached him, he stretched out a hand, and we shook.

"Well, you look like shit," my old friend said.

I smirked and slid into the opposite side of the booth, the tension in my shoulders releasing a fraction. "Thanks."

Hap took his seat again. "No, I mean it as a compliment. It's not an easy thing to achieve when your natural appearance puts male models to shame. You must be going for a world record on sleepless nights."

"You're so full of shit." I laughed. "It's that obvious huh? Listen... I've been wanting to talk to you, to apologize. I don't know what to say—"

"Do you love her?" Hap asked bluntly.

Stunned by the direct question, I hesitated. I'd hoped we might ease into this.

At least we were in a public place where the exchange wouldn't escalate into a fist fight... probably.

Pam Nookson, the owner of Nooky's, appeared tableside with a pitcher of ice water and a friendly smile. She wore a t-shirt bearing the diner's slogan and a red pencil tucked into her short pouf of blonde hair.

"Welcome to Nooky's." She set two menus on the table and filled the empty glasses in front of us. "Can I get you boys something to drink besides water?"

"I'll have some iced tea," Hap said.

"Water's fine for me."

"Okay, hon, I'll be right back with your tea and get your orders."

As soon as she was out of earshot, I answered Hap.

"I do. I love her."

Hap leaned back in the booth, crossing his arms over his chest and studying my face. "When did all this happen?"

"Nothing actually happened until we'd been on the island a while." Then I decided to drop all attempts at a defense. "But I always liked her, even back in high school."

He sat forward again. "You did? Why didn't you tell me?"

I dropped my chin and shot my friend the *Are you fucking kidding me?* look.

"Maybe it had something to do with all the death threats you were tossing around," I said. "Besides, she was just a kid back then. At that age, the difference between a senior and a sophomore is pretty extreme. Then she went off to Hollywood to do *Just Jade*, and the point was moot. Why cause trouble if I could avoid it?"

"I always knew she had a crush on you, but I had no idea you were into her."

My tone was defensive. "I didn't plan it. I tried to fight it as hard as I could, but... I don't know... she's just... perfect. I'm not sure exactly at which point I fell in love with her, but... I did."

Hap lifted his drink, took a swallow and set it down. "So... what are you doing here then?"

"What do you mean? I'm talking to you, trying to apologize."

"Duh. I mean why did you let her leave? Why are you telling *me* you love my sister instead of telling *her*? She flew out to Italy this morning believing you don't really care."

I studied my friend. "I can't believe what I'm hearing—or that you're so calm about this. What happened?"

Hap smiled. "Well, let's see... first Jessica read me the riot act about interfering in her love life. Then she informed me that you were the 'perfect gentleman' on the island and that I was a 'big, fatheaded bully' for accusing you of seducing her. And then, on the way to the airport this morning, she told me she was madly in love with you and that you were 'the one' *and* that if you and she didn't end up together, she'd hold me personally responsible and make me explain to my future children why their unmarried Aunt Jessica was bitter and angry at all the family holidays."

I couldn't help it. I laughed.

Hap went on. "But what really happened was that once I had time to think about it and get over my panic about the kidnapping, I realized there's no one I'd rather see her with. I mean, it's hard to accept the idea of my little sister with *any* guy, but you are the best guy I've ever known. I understand why she loves you. And I *know* you'll treat her right—because if you don't, I'm gonna beat your pretty face seven ways to Sunday."

The two of us laughed then locked hands. Then we stood and embraced, laughing some more and slapping each other on the back.

"Your blessing means the world to me," I said. "Now—I've got to go catch a flight and find out if I've screwed up and lost your sister for good."

TWENTY-NINE

King Frog

Thanks to the *joys* of international travel and the massive crowd, the show had already begun by the time I arrived in Venice.

The concert venue was like none I'd ever seen. The stage wasn't tucked amongst the historic buildings of the city itself but floating in the Venetian lagoon, moored in front of the Piazza San Marco.

High scaffolding on either side of the platform held massive speakers and video screens.

Speakers lined the front of the stage as well. Bright lights shone on Jade's band and the beautiful singer herself, who wore a sparkling short romper decorated in a vertical stripe pattern with green and black sequins.

A standing-room-only crowd filled the piazza. The air buzzed with excited chatter in a variety of languages.

Between the city and the floating stage, boats of every imaginable shape and size bobbed on the Venetian lagoon. Gondolas snugged up to party barges. Fishing boats floated around pocket yachts like little Remora fish orbiting whales.

I stared across the two-hundred-yard distance between the

piazza where I stood and the floating stage where Jessica was performing. The saying "so close and yet so far" had never been more apropos.

She had let all my calls go to voicemail and hadn't returned my texts or emails. I recalled her words—"If you want to see me, you can buy a ticket like everyone else."

Well, this concert was free, but at the moment I had no better chance of speaking to her in person than any of the other three hundred thousand or so spectators. Which meant I needed to find a way to get to that stage.

It was the only thing I could think of that would make her listen to me. And maybe, if I was really lucky, make her say, "yes."

Watercraft had begun pulling up to the barricade lines this morning. Now, they surrounded the stage like an armada. Even if I'd been able to find an available boat at this late hour, getting through the floating blockade would have been impossible.

There *was* a temporary pontoon bridge stretching from the piazza to the stage, and a few pedestrian stragglers still crossed it—probably VIPs who'd paid a fortune to sit on a platform directly in front of the stage.

The walkway was lined with police and private uniformed guards. There were a *lot* of them. On one hand, that pleased me. Jessica was taking her safety seriously. On the other, it was going to make things damn difficult.

Approaching one of the guards, I showed the man my business card and ID, explaining I'd been in charge of Jessica's security in the States and that I'd like to cross the walkway to the stage.

The guy waved me off, speaking in perfect English. "Nice try buddy. Now move along and enjoy the show."

Fantastico.

It was poetic justice, really. Thanks to my own stupidity,

Jessica had fired my company and gotten her own security personnel. None of these guys knew me from Adam.

The guard was armed, so I didn't argue. I did reach in my pocket and extract the small velvet box I'd brought along. Turning to a female officer, I opened the box and showed her the ring. I explained his situation to her, that I was Jessica's... uh, Jade's ex, and that I was there to propose and beg her to take me back.

The woman narrowed her eyes first at the ring then at my face. She also spoke in English but with a heavy Italian accent. "I saw the video from Coachella. Jade has a lot of stalkers—you might be one of them."

"Actually, I was her bodyguard that night," I corrected.

The woman scowled. "Even worse. You let her get kidnapped. If you really *are* a... friend of hers..." The guard's expression showed her extreme doubt. "... then you can just see her after the show at her hotel."

"Okay thanks," I said and walked away, momentarily defeated.

Obviously, I wouldn't be crossing the footbridge.

But I couldn't wait until after the show. It was highly unlikely I'd be able to get any closer to Jessica at her hotel anyway—if I could even figure out which one it was.

No, it had to be now—here—in public. The only thing I had left to offer Jessica was my complete and utter humility.

And I could think of no better way to humiliate myself than to propose to her onstage during a live, internationally televised show.

First I had to get to that stage. The bridge was a no-go. Boating there was out. There was only one way left to reach her. My experience as a navy combat diver was about to come in *very* handy.

Fishing a discarded sandwich bag from an overflowing trash can, I wrapped and sealed the contents of my pockets inside of it. Then I walked far enough away from the footbridge that the security officers wouldn't see me.

I stood at the edge of the dark lagoon. It wasn't exactly famous for its cleanliness, but I couldn't be picky. I waded in.

It was night, and I was wearing all black, so it wasn't likely I'd be spotted while swimming to the stage, but I dived far beneath the surface anyway.

There were police boats with armed officers patrolling the water. A gunshot wound would put a serious kink into my romantic proposal plans.

To be competitive during the SEAL fitness tests, I'd had to swim five hundred yards in about eight minutes, so the two-hundred-yard distance from the shore to the stage took me less than four minutes. I surfaced for air only once.

Darkness was much more of an issue than distance. While the night was good for cover, it wasn't so great for navigation. I had none of my gear with me, so I had to make a guess at my exact location in the lagoon.

I resurfaced inside the police line near the stage and *right next to* a police boat. Not good. Taking a breath, I dived again and this time swam around to the back of the stage where I'd have a better chance of climbing up undetected.

When my head broke the surface again, I heard Jessica's voice. She was introducing a new song. I treaded the dark water, listening.

"I just wrote this one," she told the audience. "It's about the relationship I just got out of. You guys know I've kissed a lot of frogs, right?"

She laughed, and the crowd cheered. There were shouts of "I love you Jade," and "I'll kiss you."

"I love you too," she said back before going on with her story. "This last one I think deserves the title of King Frog. I really loved him, but he didn't love me back... not enough anyway. It's called 'Fool Me Twice.' I hope you all like it."

As I began to pull myself from the water onto the back of the floating stage, her band began to play. Jessica's sweet voice floated across the water to my ears.

Then it struck me in the gut. Because the lyrics were about *me*.

At sixteen I gave you my heart/
You gave it back with a wink and a shrug/
All these years, all these miles/
And still you had me hooked like a drug/
But now I'm older and so much wiser/
Don't believe in kissing frogs anymore/
Fairy tale's over, the prince is a liar/
Fooled me twice, not gonna fool me no more

Standing in the dark space behind the stage, dripping wet, my muscles shaking from the cold, fast swim, I considered jumping back into the water and returning to shore.

Was there any point in going onstage and proposing after hearing *that*? The blow to my heart felt worse than the bullet I'd taken in Afghanistan.

It was excruciating to hear the evidence of just how much I'd hurt her. Cold shame washed over me, leaving me more chilled than the water had.

But then, I *had* withstood shots before and come out alive. You didn't give up the war just because you lost a battle. When it came to Jessica, I'd fight until my last breath.

She was worth it. If it meant exposing my heart to the entire world, so be it.

When the song ended, I pushed past the black curtains that concealed me and walked toward her, momentarily blinded by the bright lights shining onto the stage.

"Jessica," I called out just as a member of her new security team tackled me and threw me to the stage surface with bone-jarring force.

She whirled around, her eyes going wide at the sight of my face. "Wilder? Is that you?"

Lying on my back with a two-hundred-fifty-pound man on my chest, and a hand at my throat, I did my best to answer.

"I need to talk to you," I croaked. "Please."

She had all the power now. If she truly hated me, she could simply tell the guard she didn't know me, and I'd be in cuffs and on a police boat within minutes.

"It's okay," she told the guard. "I know him. He's a... friend. You can let him go."

The guy looked up at her but didn't release his grip. "Are you sure?"

"Yes. I'm okay. I'll be okay. He wouldn't be here without a good reason."

Her voice sounded certain, but her face was colored in confusion.

I got to my feet and approached her with a nervous smile. "Thanks."

"What are you doing here, Wilder?" She glanced back over her shoulder at the crowd and those dreaded TV cameras. "I'm... kind of in the middle of something."

"I had to tell you I'm sorry. And I love you."

Drawing the Ziploc bag from my wet shirt, I opened it and retrieved the ring box. I dropped to one knee and offered it to her.

A roar of sound swelled throughout the harbor and from the piazza as one of the cameras zoomed in on the diamond and emerald ring, displaying it on the giant video screens, and the audience realized what was happening.

Jessica, on the other hand, didn't utter a peep. She just

stared at me as if she couldn't believe what her eyes were telling her.

"I'm sorry it took me this long. I've been an idiot," I confessed. "This past week without you has been miserable. I want to be with you. I'm never going to love living in the public eye, but I realized I'd rather spend every day on a reality TV show, trailed by cameras every minute, than have a peaceful, private life without you. I want you to be my wife. I want to go wherever you go and be with you every day. I want us to make a life together."

She shook her head, swallowing hard and obviously fighting tears. "You're saying all the right things, but words are cheap. They don't make dreams come true—believe me, I know. I've been trying to write my dreams into reality since I was a kid. I've finally accepted you *can't* have it all."

Oh no. She was going to turn me down. I didn't even care that it was happening on live international TV in front of millions. The only part I cared about was losing Jessica.

Rising to my feet, I reached back into the plastic bag to fish out my leather notebook. "You're wrong. You can have it all—at least you can have *my* all. If you don't believe those words, then believe *these*."

I handed her the book containing my most private thoughts and feelings, giving her the ammunition to obliterate me if she chose to.

She'd only read a few pages of it on the island, but now she had it all—all the things I'd written about her over the years, the proof that she'd always been on my mind and in my heart.

Handing over the private words was the most vulnerable thing I'd ever done.

I only hoped it would be enough.

"It's all about you," I told her. "Every word—dating back to high school."

While the fifteen-carat ring hadn't even turned her head,

Jessica cradled the beat-up notebook as if it were made of solid gold and encrusted with precious jewels.

Her gaze moved from the book in her palms up to my eyes. "You're giving it to me?"

I nodded. "Do whatever you want to with it—share it on the internet, make fun of it in the TV interviews you'll do after this, tell everyone what a stupid sap I am... not to mention what a terrible poet."

A hush fell over the crowd. It seemed all of Venice held its breath along with me.

Finally Jessica turned to her audience, speaking into her microphone.

"What do you think? Should I give 'King Frog' just one more chance?"

The silence was broken by a deafening cheer. Jessica turned back to me, beaming. "They say yes."

"And what do you say?"

"I say... third time's a charm."

She extended her left hand, laughing and crying as I slid the ring onto her finger.

Afterward we kissed, much to the delight of the crowd, save perhaps for the guy who shouted, "Marry me instead," in Italian.

When the kiss ended, Jessica grabbed my hand and pulled me to the front edge of the stage.

"I'd like everyone to meet Wilder... my fiancé. And I want y'all to know I'm working on a new song, one that'll be perfect for a wedding. I'm going to call it, 'I Will."

Epilogue

Gray

Gray Lupine

I'd been annoyed at Wilder's mandate that I bring a plus-one to the wedding, but it was turning out to be the best date I'd had in a long time.

The woman was charming, intelligent, had a wicked sense of humor, and was an enthusiastic dance partner.

She was also eighty-eight years old.

Mrs. Victoria Hood, a client of Veridian Security and a grand dame of Eastport Bay's old-money society, seemed to be having a good time as well. She'd kept me on the dance floor for most of the reception but had finally agreed to sit one out and eat a slice of wedding cake.

"I'd never heard that young woman's music before tonight, but you can bet I'll be downloading some tunes on my smartphone tomorrow," she said, gesturing with her silver fork.

I laughed, something I'd been doing all night and did frequently when I spent time with Mrs. Hood. If it weren't for the sixty-year difference in our ages, I might have sworn the two of us were soulmates.

"We can add a Bluetooth surround-sound stereo system to your estate if you like," I offered. "That way you can blast Jade's songs in your greenhouse and sitting room and even listen to them in the shower."

I'd been working exclusively on the Hood project for several weeks, installing a state-of-the-art security system in the elderly woman's Oceanview Avenue mansion as well as constructing individual anti-burglary devices to protect each relic in her treasure trove of museum-quality fine art.

The collection was the kind that needed the highest level of protection.

Luckily, I was there to provide it. In my SEAL days, I'd been the team member sent in to disable the security system or gain entry to a location that was locked down tight.

When my military career ended, I joked the only thing I was suited to do professionally was cat burglar.

But Wilder had given me the opportunity to employ my skills legitimately. Now I used my considerable knowledge of home and commercial security equipment—and the methods burglars used to defeat it—to help people *protect* their homes and property.

It was engaging work, it paid well, and every so often I met a client that made it all worthwhile, like Mrs. Hood.

She reminded me of my own grandmother whom I'd lost a few years ago. The elderly woman and I had become fast friends, and I made a point to drop in on her regularly to make sure she was okay.

"Well, I'm more into essential oil baths than showers," she told me. "A girl has to take care of her skin, you know."

A volley of fireworks burst in the sky over the seaside estate where the wedding and reception were being held.

Mrs. Hood clasped her wrinkled hands under her chin and let out a sigh of delight as she stared up at the display.

"Oh this reminds me so much of the old days. The *parties* we used to have. I wish my granddaughter Scarlett could be here. How she used to love fireworks when she was a little girl."

"I didn't know you had a granddaughter. Scarlett's a pretty name. Where does she live?" I asked.

"Florida. She's my only grandchild."

"Is she anything like you?"

"I can't rightly say. She used to be—same stubborn streak, same love of horses—we even have the same birthday. Unfortunately I haven't seen her in twenty years—not since she was five years old. That's when her parents divorced. My daughter-in-law got custody of Scarlett because of my son's constant international travel. That woman made every excuse in the world to keep Scarlett from visiting me—probably to punish him. Now he's gone, and she's the only family I have left."

"That's terrible. You must miss her so much."

"It broke my heart for sure. I've continued to send birthday gifts and written her letters over the years, but she never writes back. She might not even live there anymore. I keep hoping she'll show up on my doorstep someday... before I run out of time to get to know her."

"Awww come on now— you've got another twenty good years in you at *least*," I teased, but we both knew it probably wasn't true.

I made a mental note to speak to Wilder about the situation when he returned from his honeymoon. Maybe there was something the security firm could do to track the girl down.

Speaking of the groom, he and the new Mrs. Lowe were headed our way, holding hands and glowing brighter than the pyrotechnic display over their heads.

"There's the beautiful couple," I said, getting to my feet to shake Wilder's hand and give Jessica a peck on the cheek.

"That's what people are saying about you two," she teased me.

"Yeah, I thought I warned you about dating clients." Wilder winked and smiled widely. "Hello Mrs. Hood. Having a good time?"

"Marvelous. I haven't had this much fun in ages. And don't worry about your Mr. Lupine. He's a wolf in name only. I assure you my honor has been completely safe with him."

"Good to hear it," Wilder said with a laugh.

Turning to Jessica, Mrs. Hood complimented her dress and her music. "You have yourself a new fan. I especially like that 'Teaser' song."

"Thank you so much." Jessica grinned up at Wilder. "I kind of like it myself. It's about the first guy I ever kissed."

"And I intend to make sure he's the *last* guy you ever kiss."

Wilder brushed a sweet touch across his new wife's lips then gave her a look that actually made me blush. It was a promise crossed with a friendly threat.

As the newlyweds walked away arm-in-arm to greet other guests, I silently congratulated myself for giving Wilder the advice to follow his heart.

It was good to see my friend and boss truly happy at last—and the sweet singer-songwriter as well. Jade's song "I Will" had brought a tear to my eye during the ceremony.

When I told her so, she'd offered to write one for me one day—when I found the right girl.

If I ever found the right girl. I was about to give up hope that she was out there.

"So, what are you doing next weekend?" I asked Mrs. Hood. "I have to go to another wedding, and if you're not busy..."

She gave me a scolding look. "I *am* busy. You can't expect

to monopolize all my time you know. I have many beaus, and I have been invited to a dance at the senior center next Saturday night."

Her expression softened, and she patted my cheek with one soft hand. "Besides, you don't want to spend your weekends squiring around an old biddy like me. You're a young, handsome man, and you should be taking out some lovely young girl you can fall in love with and marry and have lots of babies with. If you can't find someone, then I'll make it my mission to find her for you."

"My, my grandma, what big plans you have." I laughed.

She joined in the laughter, picking up on my joke. "Just bring me a basket of goodies every so often, and we'll be even."

"You've got a deal. I wouldn't say no to my own happily ever after," I said. "If I can end up half as happy as Wilder is today, I'm in."

* * *

Thank you so much for reading **The Bombshell and the Bodyguard!** I hope you loved it! If you did, I would be so grateful for a review on the retailer where you purchased it. Reviews are so important to help authors grow and help other readers find great books!

There's more to love in the world of Eastport Bay. Gray's story, Scarlett and the Big Bad Billionaire, is a sexy small town fairytale retelling of Red Riding Hood and the wolf. It's available now in ebook and print and soon to come in audio!

Make sure you're on my Tru Tales mailing list so you'll be notified of all my new releases and sales. All my VIP list members get sneak peeks, bonus epilogues, funny Tru stories, and a free novella set in the Eastport Bay universe. It's like dessert for your inbox! Here's where to sign up: https://tru-taylor.com/tru-tales/

Free book

Want a free Eastport Bay story? **The Sleepless Billionaire** is a hot, funny novella set in the world of the Eastport Bay Billionaires. My VIP mailing list members get the ebook for free! Here's where to sign up: https://trutaylor.com/tru-tales/

Also by Tru Taylor

Bookworm and the Beast- A Beauty and the Beast story

Bargain with the Bachelor- A Snow White story

The Baby and the Blueblood- A Cinderella story

The Baby-whisperer and the Brute- A Rapunzel story

The Bombshell and the Bodyguard- A Frog Prince story

Scarlett and the Big Bad Billionaire— A Red Riding Hood and the Big Bad Wolf story

The Grumpy Billionaire- A Sleeping Beauty story (Reid's story)

The Merry Billionaire— A holiday novella (Hap's story)

The Sleepless Billionaire- (Tuck's story) Free when you join my VIP list!

No More Heartbreakers- A New Adult Romance

No More Billionaires- A New Adult Romance

No More Bad Boys- A New Adult Romance

About the Author

Award-winning author Tru Taylor writes small town romance that's hot and sunny and a little bit funny.

She runs on Coke Zero and dark chocolate, lives for lunches with her girlfriends, and drives to the town beach several times a week to watch the sun set over the water.

She loves LOVE and will attempt to turn any show or movie she's watching into a romance whether it is one or not. Star Wars? A romance. Lord of the Rings? Clearly a romance. The Expendables? Okay, well not even Tru can redeem that one.

When she's not writing, Tru enjoys watching movies and reading books with happy endings, spending time with her husband and two kids, and sneaking Hershey's Kisses from the top shelf of the freezer throughout the day. (Top shelf because... two kids. Enough said.)

Tru is the author of the Eastport Bay small town rom com

series and loves living in a small New England town where she's surrounded every day by the beautiful coastal setting you see brought to life in her books.

Want fun email from Tru? Join her Tru Tales mailing list for true stories of small town romantic comedy, excerpts, sneak peeks, giveaways, and a free novella set in the world of Eastport Bay! Here's where to sign up: https://trutaylor.-com/tru-tales/

The Bombshell and the Bodyguard is a work of fiction. Characters, names, places, brands, media, and incidents are either products of the author's imagination or have been used fictitiously and should not be construed as real. Any resemblance to actual persons, living or dead, events, or locales is entirely coincidental.

Oxford South Press November 2021

Editor: Judy Roth

Cover by: Emily Cover Design

www.ingramcontent.com/pod-product-compliance
Lightning Source LLC
Chambersburg PA
CBHW050849190726
48286CB00007B/2299
* 9 7 8 1 9 4 6 1 6 6 2 7 2 *